**'I thought yo—
murmured he**

'I did...I do. But—— Jane broke off and a hot
flush of shame burned her cheeks.

'But you're a nice girl who doesn't play games
with men she hardly knows,' he finished for
her.

Games? Was that all it had meant to him, that
kiss which had inflamed her, igniting all kinds
of unfamiliar passions within her?

'That's right,' she said coldly.

Dear Reader

Spring is here at last—a time for new beginnings and time, perhaps, finally to start putting all those New Year's resolutions into action! Whatever your plans, don't forget to look out this month for a wonderful selection of romances from the exotic Amazon, Australia, the Americas and enchanting Italy. Our resolution remains, as always, to bring you the best in romance from around the world!

The Editor

Angela Devine grew up in Tasmania surrounded by forests, mountains and wild seas, so she dislikes big cities. Before taking up writing, she worked as a teacher, librarian and university lecturer. As a young mother and Ph.D. student, she read romantic fiction for fun and later decided it would be even more fun to write it. She is married with four children, loves chocolate and Twinings teas and hates ironing. Her current hobbies are gardening, bushwalking, travelling and classical music.

Recent titles by the same author:

YESTERDAY'S HUSBAND

UNWELCOME INVADER

BY

ANGELA DEVINE

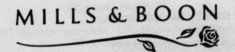

MILLS & BOON

MILLS & BOON LIMITED
ETON HOUSE, 18-24 PARADISE ROAD
RICHMOND, SURREY TW9 1SR

To L.B.

*MILLS & BOON and the Rose Device
are trademarks of the publisher.*

*First published in Great Britain 1995
by Mills & Boon Limited*

© Angela Devine 1995

*Australian copyright 1995   Philippine copyright 1995
This edition 1995*

ISBN 0 263 78929 2

*Set in Times Roman 10½ on 12 pt.
01-9504-53051 C*

Made and printed in Great Britain

CHAPTER ONE

'LOOKS as though your dad has let you down,' said Brett mildly.

Gazing up and down the rapidly emptying airport, Jane felt inclined to agree with him. It was after eleven o'clock and most of the passengers had already disappeared hurriedly into the chill autumn night. After being delayed for several hours by engine trouble in Melbourne nobody wanted to linger any further. Only a few airline employees and a single family with some problems about missing luggage were still left in the small Hobart air terminal. There was no sign of her father anywhere.

'I think you're right,' she admitted ruefully. 'Although I don't know why he hasn't shown up. I wrote to him two weeks ago and told him when I was arriving. I even reminded him to phone and check that the flight was on schedule, which it wasn't! But you know Dad...he's so unreliable. I'm afraid I won't be able to give you a ride home after all, Brett.'

'Well, it's not the end of the world, mate. Tell you what, I'll see if the bloke down at the Hertz desk can rustle up a hire-car for us, then I'll give *you* a ride home.'

'Thanks, Brett, you're a real sweetie.'

With a sigh of relief that she didn't have to make any further effort, Jane sat down in one of the blue seats with her luggage scattered untidily around her. She was almost reeling with fatigue after the long flight

5

from Thailand, the almost equally long wait in Melbourne and the final flight home to Tasmania, so that for once she was quite happy to let Brett make decisions for her. As she gazed after his stocky figure ploughing purposefully towards the car rental desk Jane smiled affectionately. Dear Brett, with his red face and thick, capable hands and milky-blond hair already growing sparse across his scalp, although he was only twenty-seven—a year older than Jane herself. What a shame it was that she could never feel anything more than a sisterly affection for him! Ever since they had started school together, more than twenty years ago, Brett had been her admirer and protector. But without that mysterious, indefinable spark she knew he would never be anything more than that. She had made that clear to him, time after time, but that didn't prevent Brett from going on hoping. In addition to being good-natured he was infinitely stubborn. A tremor of doubt went through Jane as she wondered whether it had been wise to offer him even the lukewarm encouragement of a ride home from the airport. Then she dismissed her misgiving. What else could she have done? After all, they were neighbours, with Brett's farm only two miles down the road from her own home. Besides, she had expected her father to be with them.

'All right, mate, all sorted out. Give me some of your gear and we'll get moving.'

Ten minutes later they had left the airport behind and were on the winding road which led to the small village of Richmond. Jane lolled in her seat, halfway between waking and sleeping, enjoying the peaceful, moonlit countryside which unrolled slowly past them. Brett drove at an unhurried pace, as he did everything else. She had plenty of time to admire the bare, stark branches of dead gum trees, the dense masses of living bushland, the tiny blobs of sheep as motionless as children's toys in their paddocks, the ghostly outlines of farmhouses already dark and silent for the night. Then a wind must have arisen in the west, for the sounds of rustling leaves came to them above the purr of the car's engine and scuds of flying clouds went sailing over the moon's bright face, so that for a moment the moon itself seemed to be hurtling across the dark sky. Brett drove even more slowly through the village with its sandstone Georgian buildings and carefully tended gardens. Here there were a few reassuring signs of life—firelight, street-lamps, even a snatch of laughter and music from a restaurant open late—then they were out into the stillness of the countryside again. With a quickening of her heartbeat, Jane sat forward in her seat for the first glimpse of her vineyards and the old farmhouse called Saddler's Corner where she had spent her childhood. There they were! Row upon leafy row of them, all along the river's edge and climbing the slopes of the hills beyond. The sheep which had been the mainstay of the farm for generations had all been banished to distant paddocks long ago.

'Your vines are looking good,' remarked Brett. 'I was talking to your overseer, Charlie, about a month ago, just before I went on my holidays. He said you'd be ready to harvest just after Easter.'

'That's right,' agreed Jane. 'That's why I came back, really. I was learning so much in France that I could quite happily have stayed away for another six months.'

'Well, I'm glad you didn't,' said Brett in measured tones, and let his left hand drop casually on to her knee.

Jane felt as if she were an apple or an orange being squeezed for ripeness. The sensation was not exactly unpleasant, but it woke nothing in her except embarrassment and a desire to escape.

'Don't, Brett,' she begged in a stifled voice, removing his hand.

'One of these days you'll come round,' he said good-humouredly. 'I'm not a bad bloke, Jane; I'm steady and I've got my own farm. That's worth something.'

With relief Jane saw that they had bumped up the gravel driveway and round the loop which led to the rear of the house.

'I won't ask you in, Brett,' she said hastily. 'It's rather late and I'm terribly exhausted after that long flight.'

'Sure. No worries,' agreed Brett. 'But at least let me see you inside.'

'Well, just to the back door,' agreed Jane uncomfortably. 'I'll be fine then. I see Dad's left the outside light on for me. Perhaps he didn't get the message about the plane being delayed.'

'Sure you'll be all right, then?' asked Brett, setting her bags down for her. 'Anything else I can do for you? A goodnight kiss, maybe?'

'No!' wailed Jane. 'Oh, Brett, cut it out. I'm very, very fond of you, but not like that!'

'Some women have no taste!' lamented Brett, touching her briefly on the cheek and then lumbering away to the hire-car. 'See you in a day or two, Jane.'

Tired as she was, Jane did not go inside immediately once the car had vanished. Instead she stood breathing in deep lungfuls of the clean, cold night air with its unmistakable Australian smell of eucalyptus. From somewhere out of sight she could hear the hoarse croaking of frogs, and the sudden hiss and scuffle and a flash of red eyes in the gum trees next to the barn told her that the possums were active tonight. An exultant smile curved Jane's lips. It was good to be back! And the best thing of all was the thought that her vines were nearly ready for their first harvest ...

Suddenly she realised that she couldn't possibly wait until tomorrow morning to see how the grapes were getting along. She would have to take a quick glance right away. Groping in her handbag, she fished out the small torch which she always carried while travelling and trained its circle of light on the path leading down to the first of the vineyards. As she picked her way through the rows of espaliered vines a feeling of mounting pride and delight rose inside her. Soon, very soon, she would have her first harvest and then she would find out just what kind of wine she could make from her own grapes. Reaching out, she plucked one of them from a dark cluster and put it in her mouth. It burst with a faint pop, releasing a cool liquid on her tongue—full-bodied, still slightly acid, but very, very promising. With a contented sigh Jane spat the pips on the ground and picked her way back up the slope towards the cluster of buildings. Perhaps she would just take a quick look at her wine cellar too, before she went to bed.

The wine cellar was located beneath the big stone building which had originally been a dairy and was

now used to store all the paraphernalia of the
vineyard. Disliking the thought of the bright glare of
fluorescent lights, Jane did not flick the switch, but
used her torch to guide her past the dark shapes of
picking buckets, secateurs and lengths of irrigation
pipe to the stairs which led to the next level. The door
at the bottom was padlocked, but she had the
necessary key on her keyring. A moment later the door
creaked open and she stepped inside and flashed her
torch around. There was a row of oak barrels with
silicon bungs—empty now but soon to be filled with
her own wine—and a long row of weldmesh shelves
containing her own collection of Australian wines built
up over several years. It occurred to her that it would
be nice to have a glass of wine to celebrate her return.
She could always invite a friend over to lunch
tomorrow, to finish the bottle with her. Pausing
pleasurably, she ran her fingers along the mesh and
finally chose a bottle of Penfold's Grange Hermitage.
Her mouth watered at the prospect of that dark berry
fruit and charred oak bouquet, the full-bodied flavour
and the astringent tannins that would follow.

'I can't wait,' she murmured aloud.

At that moment there was a stealthy footstep on
the stairs behind her. Not particularly troubled, Jane
swung round, expecting to see her father. Instead a
total stranger stood there before her, caught in the
beam of her torch. A grim, unsmiling man in his mid-
thirties, dressed in grey trousers and an open necked
shirt, with dark brown hair brushed back from a lean,
sardonic face and the most hostile brown eyes Jane
had ever seen. He was advancing towards her in a
purposeful crouch like a hunting animal and there was

something utterly terrifying about the grim twist of his lips. Jane's heart lurched.

'What do you want?' she asked in a high, nervous voice, stepping back a pace and half raising the bottle as if it was a weapon.

'You,' he breathed, and sprang.

Jane screamed, hurled the bottle and ran. There was wild confusion as she heard the shatter of breaking glass against the brick wall, smelled the sudden, heady perfume of red wine and felt her heart would burst from her chest as she raced down the avenue of flagstones between the shelves and the barrels. Her torch beam swung wildly, revealing the other exit, a crude, wooden door leading out into a rough shrubbery on the slope behind the building. It shouldn't be padlocked, only bolted from the inside. Could she make it before he caught her? Transferring the torch to her left hand, she seized the bolt with her right, wrenched violently and pushed. It was like a nightmare. Nothing happened. Some resistance on the outside was preventing the door from opening. With a sob of frustration Jane hurled herself at it. A shuddering jolt went through her entire body, but still the door would not yield. Then suddenly a powerful hand caught her by the neck of her shirt and swung her round.

'It seems I have you right where I want you,' breathed a hoarse, masculine voice.

'Oh, no, you don't!' cried Jane defiantly and, swinging the torch, she hit him hard on the side of the face. Another jarring impact travelled up Jane's arm, but the stranger barely seemed to feel the blow. The only response he gave was a quick, sharp intake of breath, then his right hand came out and crushed her fingers, forcing her to release the torch. Gasping in outrage, Jane kicked him in the shins. With a faint sigh, he took one of her hands and twisted it behind her back. A warning twinge of pain went through her.

'I don't want to hurt you, *mademoiselle*,' he murmured apologetically. 'But you and I need to have a little talk.'

'What about?' panted Jane indignantly. 'What is there to talk about? You're a raving lunatic who attacked me for no reason at all.'

He shone the torch disconcertingly in her face, so that she blinked in its dazzling light.

'Quite pretty,' he said in the tone of a connoisseur. 'Big green eyes, delicate features, long, curly blonde hair. The hair needing the attentions of a good hairdresser. Not quite the sort of vandal I expected, I must admit. Tell me, *mademoiselle*, what made you break into my wine cellar?'

'Y-your wine cellar?' stuttered Jane furiously. 'Now I know you're insane. This is my wine cellar, not yours.'

'Ah, I begin to understand,' he said courteously. 'You are not the juvenile delinquent, but merely deranged. My apologies for handling you so roughly, *mademoiselle*. You deserve pity, not blame.'

'I am not a juvenile delinquent!' shouted Jane, although as a matter of fact she looked remarkably like one in her crumpled jeans and wine-splashed shirt with her hair falling in her eyes. 'And I'm not mentally deranged, either! If anyone is deranged it's you, claiming that this wine cellar is yours. My father is the legal owner of this farm and I own every barrel and bottle of wine in this cellar.'

As she spoke she slapped one hand against the weldmesh shelves, to emphasise her point.

'Don't do that!' exclaimed her companion in horror. 'It's very bad for the wine.'

'I know that!' snapped Jane. 'I'm a winemaker. Why on earth would you think I was a delinquent?'

He shrugged.

'My apologies. I've had some trouble with vandals since I took possession of the vineyard here.'

'Took possession of the vineyard?' echoed Jane in bewilderment. 'I don't understand! Have I wandered into some kind of crazy nightmare?'

'There does seem to be some confusion,' agreed the stranger tranquilly. 'You said that your father owns this property. What is his name?'

There was an air of authority in his voice that made Jane answer without hesitation.

'Colin West.'

'And your name, *mademoiselle*?'

'Jane West.'

'*Bon*. We begin to make progress. Allow me to introduce myself. I am Marc Le Rossignol.'

'How do you do?' said Jane with heavy sarcasm.

'Ah, you are thinking perhaps that this is no place for exchanging the pleasantries? How right you are, Miss West. Why don't you come inside and we'll discuss the matter in comfort?'

'Inside?' echoed Jane in horror. 'Do you mean you're staying here? Are you some kind of guest of my father's?'

'Not exactly,' replied Marc. 'We are more in the nature of business associates, but I'll explain all that once we're inside.'

Jane glared at him suspiciously in the inadequate torchlight. Something very odd was going on here, but at least it no longer looked as if this Marc Le Rossignol was some kind of mad rapist or burglar. Suddenly she made up her mind.

'All right,' she agreed curtly. 'I don't suppose I can come to much harm anyway with my father in the house.'

Marc shrugged.

'Unfortunately your father is not in the house,' he replied. 'He has gone to New Zealand.'

'New Zealand?' exclaimed Jane. 'That's the first I've heard about it! I don't have the faintest idea of what's going on here.'

'Nor I, *mademoiselle*,' replied Marc briskly. 'But perhaps we can get to the bottom of it all over a meal and a glass of wine.'

Jane sighed. Her head was spinning. After the long flight and the drama of the last few minutes the last thing she wanted to do was share a meal with this unwelcome invader, whoever he was. Yet obviously she would get no peace until matters were straightened out.

'All right,' she agreed ungraciously.

With a proprietorial gesture, which annoyed her intensely, Marc took the torch and guided her with exaggerated courtesy back along the way they had come. At the foot of the stairs Jane crouched down amid the broken glass and the spilt wine and sorrowfully picked up a shattered fragment of the bottle which still had the label adhering to it.

'Grange Hermitage,' she said tragically, shaking her head. 'What a waste! It's enough to make a girl weep.'

'Or a man,' agreed Marc gloomily. 'But I've got something equally fine inside. A bottle of Petrus 1985. I look forward to hearing your opinion of it.'

In a daze, Jane allowed herself to be hustled inside the house. In the outside porch Marc halted as if noticing something for the first time, and then strode across to the patch of shadow where Jane had dumped her luggage.

'These are your bags, one assumes?' he asked.

'Yes.'

'Strange.'

With a Gallic shrug he moved towards the back door, making no attempt to pick up the bags. Obviously he was either too ill-mannered to help her or had no intention of letting her stay the night! Darting him a smouldering look, Jane snatched them up herself.

'What are you doing with those?' he demanded.

'What does it look as if I'm doing? I'm staying here. This is my home.'

He smiled faintly, a smile that struck Jane as being oddly dangerous. Suave, mockingly amused, but with a hint of some indefinable wildness and power behind it. To her surprise he suddenly took both bags out of her hands.

'How pleasant. It will be very agreeable to have some feminine company. One always misses the gentle voices, the elegant clothes, the charming manners of women.'

Since Jane's voice so far had been shrill with indignation, her clothes were travel-stained and splashed with wine and her manner was hostile to the point of rudeness, she had little doubt that this infuriating stranger was mocking her. Enraged beyond belief, she could not even think of a snappy comeback, but simply stood glaring at him as he held open the mesh door for her by leaning against it with one powerful shoulder.

'Do come in,' he urged pleasantly, as if he was a host welcoming a favourite guest. 'If you're going to stay the night then I'll need to arrange some things for you. A bath, a meal, a bedroom.'

Jane stepped inside, as aggressively as if she were laying a territorial claim to an entire continent. Then she further relieved her feelings by turning and kicking the massive cedar door shut behind her. After that she swung round, planted her hands on her hips and addressed herself to the stranger.

'Now look here, Mr Le Rossignol or whatever your name is.'

'Marc, please,' he murmured. 'You Australians are so informal, aren't you? Since I'm staying in your country it's only polite that I follow your customs. And perhaps I may call you Jane?'

'You may call me anything you like as long as you get out of my house,' flared Jane. 'And the sooner the better. But first will you kindly tell me what's going on here?'

'All in good time,' he replied tranquilly. 'First you will wish to tidy up and have something to eat. Your clothes—they are only fit to throw away.'

Jane glared at him. She didn't feel at all sure that he was referring only to the splashes of wine on her clothes. Something in the disapproving lift of his eyebrows as he scanned her body made her feel that he did not approve of women who travelled in faded old jeans and cheap, green cotton windcheaters. Well, she didn't care whether he approved of her or not! How dared he stand there looking her up and down as if she were something on sale and not a very good bargain at that?

It only annoyed her further to realise that he seemed to have come off completely unscathed when she flung the bottle of wine at him. He must have been still on the stairs and therefore protected from the impact when it shattered against the wall of the cellar itself. Thinking it over, Jane was of course extremely relieved to realise that the bottle hadn't hit him, causing heaven knew what serious injuries. All the same, she wouldn't have minded in the least if the immaculate perfection of his striped blue and white shirt and grey, pleated trousers had been gloriously splattered with stains that would be almost impossible to remove.

It wasn't just this baffling situation that made her dislike him so much. It was something about his manner—so smooth, so confident, so certain that he could control the world and everybody in it. Being so good-looking probably had something to do with his aura of power and authority. He was a shade over six feet, with powerful shoulders, narrow hips and hard, muscular thighs, but it was his face that commanded most attention. The tough jaw, the shrewdly narrowed brown eyes, the mocking smile and the rather rugged features gave the irresistible impression of a man born to win. He seemed unaware of her hostile scrutiny as he glanced down at the labels on her bags.

'You've had a long journey, *mademoiselle*. All the way from Thailand today.'

'Longer than that, really,' she said. 'I only stayed one night in Bangkok to break my journey.'

'And before that you were . . . where?'

'France,' she replied.

'Ah, my own country. Excellent. We will have a discussion about it over our supper. But first you will want to have a bath.'

He set down the bags, strode further into the hall, opened the big linen closet and handed her a huge, fluffy white towel, a bath mat and a washcloth.

'The bathroom is the second door on the left,' he said.

'I know where the bathroom is!' flared Jane.

'Of course, of course,' he murmured in an amused voice. 'Well, then, I'll leave you to it while I go and heat up some food.'

Jane was quietly seething as she stalked into the bathroom and began to run hot water into the old claw-footed bath. How dared this stranger treat her like a guest in her own home? And what was he doing here? The questions buzzed in her head like a cloud of hornets, but the whole evening was beginning to take on a dreamy, surrealist air, like some sort of strange nightmare. Yet the clouds of steam rising from the bath and the fragrant horse-chestnut scent of Badedas were real enough, even if the tiled floor did seem to be undulating gently underneath her feet. With a wail of exhaustion Jane stamped out into the hall, snatched up the smaller of her two bags and re-treated to the bathroom. As she locked the door, she wished she could just escape from the whole crazy predicament. All she wanted to do now was soak in the hot, foamy water, then dry off and stumble up to bed. Instead she had to try and clear her tired brain enough to go out and do battle with this extraordinary foreigner who seemed to have taken over her home.

Deliberately she kept him waiting, but the results were not helpful. She almost fell asleep in the soothing hot water and was roused from a drifting doze by a peremptory hammering on the door.

'Have you drowned in there?' demanded a deep, masculine voice. 'Must I come in and rescue you? I can break the lock if you're in difficulties.'

Alarmed at the threat, Jane scrambled out of the bath and began hastily to dress. Once she was dry she hesitated in front of the mirror, then wiped off the steamy glass with her towel and looked at herself critically. If she had been alone, she would have put on comfortable old pyjamas and some sheepskin boots. As it was, she paused indecisively. Should she put on an even older pair of clean jeans and a more ragged windcheater as an act of defiance, or dress up to the nines?

From childhood onwards Jane had always tried to tackle difficult situations by making sure that she looked her very, very best. Somehow it always helped to control those butterflies of insecurity in her stomach. But if she dressed nicely mightn't this arrogant stranger think that she was trying to lead him on? She stared at herself in the mirror. Long, curly blonde hair, wide green eyes, heart-shaped face with a small pointy chin and a wide, defiant mouth.

'Why should I care what he thinks?' she demanded aloud. 'I'll wear whatever I like!'

Kneeling down, she unzipped her bag and took out clean underwear, tights, shoes and the one wild extravagance of her French trip—a dress of pale green clinging georgette, which clung to the curves of her body and made her look ten thousand times more sexy and sophisticated than she ever usually did. Jane scrambled into these clothes, brushed her hair, sprayed herself with Arpège, fastened a gold and pearl-drop necklace around her throat and applied a glossy scarlet lipstick to her lips. Then, squaring her shoulders and ready to do battle, she opened the bathroom door and charged.

'Go into the dining-room,' called a masculine voice, which was already beginning to be hatefully familiar. 'I'll be with you in a moment.'

Jane gasped as she entered the dining-room. The large cedar dining-table that she and her father only ever bothered to set for special occasions like Christmas dinner was covered with an exquisite lace tablecloth. At one end two places were set; candles burned in silver candelabra and their gentle, flickering light winked off crystal glasses, heavy silver cutlery and the best Wedgwood china. Mouth-watering scents drifted in from the kitchen. Some kind of delicious beef stew, with an undertone of other delights. Fresh bread and something fruity and spicy. An apple tart perhaps? Jane's spirits revived magically. She might be small and even rather frail-looking, but she had a formidable appetite. Perhaps there was something to be said for having mad Frenchmen take over the house if they cooked like this!

A moment later the mad Frenchman entered the dining-room. He paused at the sight of Jane and a small, approving smile lit his face.

'Very chic,' he murmured. 'I congratulate you, *mademoiselle*. I half expected you to appear looking like a grape-picker after the harvest.'

Jane flushed, torn between pleasure and annoyance.

'Can I do anything to help in the kitchen?' she asked.

'But no, it is all organised. I had only to heat things up. Have a glass of sherry and I'll bring in the soup.'

He moved across to the sideboard and turned back to look enquiringly at her as his hand hovered above the bottles.

'A medium dry Reynella, please,' she said.

'A very good choice. I think I'll join you. Now, please sit down at the table and we'll eat.'

Jane sipped the pale, straw-coloured, nutty-flavoured liquid and stared wonderingly after Marc's departing back as he vanished into the kitchen. Moments later he returned, first with a couple of hot bread rolls in a napkin and then with two bowls of clear soup.

'Consommé Julienne,' he announced, setting one down in front of her.

'*Bon appetit*,' said Jane automatically.

'Ah, you speak French?' asked Marc with interest.

'Not really,' she replied. 'Certainly not fluently, but I've just spent six months in the Champagne district.'

'Really? What were you doing there?'

'Learning more about winemaking.'

'And is this a hobby, or your profession?'

'My profession,' said Jane proudly.

'You've trained in it?'

'Yes. After I finished school I did a winemaking course in South Australia, worked for a year at Penfold's and then came back here to Tasmania to try and start a family vineyard. That was five years ago.'

'So it's your hand that's been at work planting the vines and setting up the equipment? Are you the one who masterminded the whole enterprise?'

'Yes,' agreed Jane with satisfaction. 'I put in Riesling and Cabernet Shiraz vines several years ago. Since then I've planted and pruned and irrigated. It's been hard work, although I've had some help from my father and from Charlie Kendall, who works for us. In fact, Charlie became so good at handling everything that I felt I could afford to go to France for six months to learn more about the trade.'

'You've done well,' said Marc. 'It's an impressive little operation, although it would have been wise to put more nets over the vines. It protects them from birds and prevents the risk of botrytis.'

'You know about wines yourself, then?' asked Jane, intrigued in spite of herself.

'It's in the blood,' replied Marc. 'My family have been winemakers near Bordeaux for the last five hundred years.'

'Then what on earth are you doing here?' demanded Jane in a baffled voice.

'All in good time,' he said, rising to his feet. 'Have you finished your soup? May I take your bowl?'

After he had vanished into the kitchen again, Jane sipped her sherry and frowned thoughtfully. There was a mystery about Marc that intrigued her. Who was he? What was he doing here? If they had met in different circumstances, she might have found him fascinating. As it was, she felt very, very troubled and uneasy.

A moment later he returned and set a bubbling iron casserole on to a hot pad. Jane inhaled ecstatically, revelling in the mingled odours of stewed beef, red wine, bayleaf, black pepper.

'*Boeuf à la bourguignonne,*' she breathed.

'Ah, your nose does not fail you,' said Marc. 'But the real test is with the wine. Tell me what you think of this.'

He fetched a decanter from the sideboard and poured a small quantity of purplish-red liquid into the bottom of Jane's crystal wine glass. She raised it to her nose, inhaled, swirled and then drank.

'It's magnificent!' she said. 'Very rich and well-balanced, with a lace-like finesse and incredible ripe fruit aromas.'

'Quite right,' he agreed. 'You've learned a lot in France.'

Jane helped herself to a substantial serving of the stew, accompanied by waxy new potatoes and carrots in a herb butter. For the moment she had almost forgotten her dislike and distrust of Marc Le Rossignol.

'Oh, I did,' she agreed eagerly. 'It's an amazing place; there's so much skill, so much dedication, so much tradition. The French winemakers are wonderful.'

'Ah, yes. But where there is appreciation there must also be a faculty for criticism,' said Marc. 'What did you find to criticise there?'

'Well——' said Jane doubtfully.

'Please, don't spare my feelings. Be perfectly frank with me.'

'Perhaps too much emphasis on tradition,' she said. 'Sometimes they seem a little hidebound, unwilling to try new things.'

'I couldn't agree with you more. Australian winemakers are often more adventurous, more willing to use new technology. I think Australia is a very exciting place at the moment for anyone seriously interested in wine. That's why I'm here.'

Jane put down her fork and gave him a troubled look.

'Why are you here?' she demanded bluntly.

With another of his mocking smiles, Marc changed the subject.

'Are you fond of cooking?' he asked.

Jane was annoyed but decided not to pursue the subject further, at least for the moment. Yet all her initial dislike of Marc Le Rossignol came surging back at full strength. During the remainder of the meal she confined herself to terse replies to his questions. Her only weak moment came when Marc produced a pear and brown sugar tart that was so good she had to acknowledge it.

'That was superb,' she said grudgingly. 'Can you always produce a three-course meal at a moment's notice?'

Marc smiled.

'Usually,' he agreed. 'I'm fond of good food and fortunately I had some substantial leftovers from last night's meal. Also fortunately, I was too busy to eat anything much earlier this evening.'

'Too busy doing what?' asked Jane.

Their eyes met.

'You've bathed, you've eaten,' said Marc, as if he were a doctor assessing a patient's progress. 'I think perhaps you're ready to face the truth now. Come into the sitting-room and we'll have our little discussion.'

Hardly able to contain her alarm, Jane followed him into the sitting-room next door. There was a fire burning in the fireplace and the room seemed comfortably inviting with its smell of lemon furniture polish, woodsmoke and old leather couches. There were no curtains but cedar shutters kept out the chill night air, and the faded Persian rug on the floor, with its now dim patterns of scarlet and royal blue, looked reassuringly familiar. The grandfather clock in the hall ticked stoically and then struck once with a reverberating boom as Jane lowered herself into a comfortable chintz armchair by the fire. One a.m. Somehow the sound had an oddly sinister ring, as if it heralded the end of everything she had ever known and loved, as if this man had come like some dangerous enchanter to change her world forever. A feeling of growing alarm clamoured inside her.

'What are you doing here?' she burst out. 'Why have you taken over my home?'

'It's very simple,' said Marc, standing with one arm draped along the mantelpiece. 'You really are Colin West's daughter, aren't you?'

'Yes.'

'Well, I can't imagine why your father hasn't told you this, but it seems I must be the one to do so. There have been some big changes here. In the first place your father has sold off all his sheep. Secondly...' He paused.

'Secondly?' prompted Jane with an ominous sense of misgiving.

'I have leased this property from him with an option to purchase at any time during the next three months.'

Jane gasped as the implications of his words slowly sank in.

'You mean...you could buy this place any time you want to in the next three months?'

'Exactly,' agreed Marc.

For a moment Jane was shocked speechless.

'The house? The vineyards? The outhouses...everything?' she stammered at last.

'Everything,' he agreed gravely.

Suddenly Jane's disbelief was replaced by anger—hot and rich and murderous.

'But that's ridiculous!' she cried wildly, jumping to her feet. 'This has been my home ever since I was born. And the vineyards, the winemaking plant...' Her voice broke. 'What happens to those?'

Marc's face was inscrutable. With the firelight leaping over his features he looked uncannily like some stage demon.

'All fixed property is included in the sale,' he said in measured tones. 'Naturally that means all of the vineyards and most of the winemaking plant. Movable property may be taken with you, but that won't be much. Only the wine collection, the empty barrels, the ladders, buckets, a few pruning shears. The rest will all be mine if I decide to go ahead with the purchase.'

Jane stumbled desperately across the room, hot tears stinging behind her eyes, then she turned on him like an animal at bay.

'That's impossible! I was the one who put up the money for most of this. I had a legacy from my grandmother and I spent every cent of it on this place. My father can't just sell it behind my back without my approval!'

Marc shrugged. His voice was very calm and cool and seemed to come from a great distance.

'I checked the legal details very carefully before I entered into this contract. I always do. There is no doubt that your father is the legal owner of this property, nor that it is unencumbered by any mortgages. These payments you say you made on the vine-yards, the wine plant . . . have you any proof of this?'

Jane was furious at his sceptical tone.

'I don't just say I made the payments!' she shouted. 'I did make them!'

Marc's voice continued relentlessly, as if he had scarcely heard her impassioned interruption.

'No doubt you have documents to prove this?'

Jane's head swam with exhaustion and disbelief.

'Yes. No. Not exactly. After I inherited the money from my grandmother my father persuaded me to form a company. It was all terribly complicated.'

'Not Saddler's Vineyards Limited, by any chance?' asked Marc in a hushed voice.

'Yes,' said Jane uneasily.

'*Parbleu*!' exclaimed Marc, leaving his place by the mantelpiece and crossing the room to her. 'I'm extremely sorry for you, Jane. It seems to me that your father has . . . what's the expression you Australians use? . . . sold you down the river. I've seen the documents governing the formation of that company. Your father is chief managing director and has a controlling interest in it. You were a very foolish girl to hand over control of your assets to another person in such a manner. What possessed you to do such a thing?'

Jane's head came up and her eyes blazed. Her blonde hair seemed to crackle around her shoulders with a life of its own.

'Because I trusted him!' she cried. 'OK? I trusted him! He's my father, for heaven's sake. He wouldn't do a thing like this to me.'

'Wouldn't he?' asked Marc quietly.

With a low groan Jane crossed to the fireplace and stood staring unseeingly into the leaping flames. Certain bitter memories of her mother came back to her.

'Maybe he would,' she admitted at last in a defeated voice. 'Oh, not deliberately, I suppose. He'd feel certain that he was doing the right thing and he'd excuse it to himself somehow. Tell himself that he was going to make huge profits for me by putting it into some harebrained scheme of his own. My mother always complained that he ran through all her money before they split up. I used to think it was just bitterness, but now I'm not sure... Are you telling me that I'm financially ruined?'

'Only if I go ahead with the purchase of this property,' said Marc. 'If I don't, there's a chance you might regain control of your assets.'

Jane swung round.

'Then don't do it!' she cried passionately. 'Please, please don't do it! You said yourself it's an impressive little vineyard and I've worked hard on it. Don't make me give it up.'

Marc shook his head fastidiously.

'Why should it matter to me?' he asked.

CHAPTER TWO

'BECAUSE it's a question of simple decency!' cried Jane.

Marc gave her a baffled look, as if he had never heard the word in his life.

'I still don't see what it has to do with me,' he said dismissively. 'Obviously, the first thing we need to do is phone your father tomorrow morning in New Zealand and find out exactly what the legal position is.'

'Legal position!' protested Jane. 'That's all that matters to you, isn't it? The legal position! Don't you have any feelings at all?'

Marc's face remained completely impassive. Only the eyes seemed alive—dark, brooding, thoughtful. But his face might have been carved out of granite for all the encouragement it gave her.

'This is nothing but a business transaction to me,' he said. 'I've made an extremely generous payment to your father for the option to purchase this property. I've also had to make extensive arrangements in France to cover my absence in Australia for three months. Why should I throw away all that when there's no certainty that I could even help you by doing so?'

Jane gave a defeated sigh. He was quite right. Why should he? After all, it was her own stupid fault she was in this position, although that didn't make it any easier to bear. Quite the reverse, in fact. She felt shaken, humiliated, betrayed. And instead of making some attempt to comfort her this unfeeling stranger simply stood there, staring at her as impassively as a judge.

'What are you going to do with the place if you do buy it?' she demanded accusingly. 'Winemaking here is a lot different from in France.'

He smiled with unexpected charm.

'That's half the attraction for me,' he said. 'I want to be one of the flying winemakers. It's tremendous good luck that the seasons are reversed in the two hemispheres. By spending half the year in Europe and half the year in Australia I can have two vintages. Twice the chance to make superb wine, plus the best of French tradition and Australian innovation. It seems ideal to me.'

'And you're prepared to ruin me to do it?' demanded Jane bitterly.

'You're being melodramatic, *chérie*. You're not ruined yet. And even if you were, it would be entirely your own doing. You've been a naïve, impetuous little fool, you know.'

Jane caught her breath sharply and clenched her fists.

'You patronising——! I hate you. I wish you'd never come here!'

'I begin to wish it myself,' murmured Marc as he met her scowling gaze. 'You have no manners at all, *mademoiselle*. You attack me with bottles and torches—what next will it be? A pitchfork? Or just your own teeth and claws? Now that might be interesting.'

Something in that husky drawl sent a throb of unwilling excitement through Jane's body, which only annoyed her still further. She made an impatient movement towards the door but found that Marc was blocking her way. He made no attempt to move, but simply stood there—large, threatening and intensely masculine. She paused, irresolute, not wanting to make an undignified and very obvious detour around him, but the pause was a mistake. Looking up into those mocking brown eyes, she was suddenly conscious of another reluctant thrill of attraction to him, of an electric tingling in her limbs that filled her with an insane urge to move into his arms. The scent of his cologne, spicy and erotic, drifted into her nostrils and her senses swam. Horrified, she broke away and retreated to the door.

'Don't worry!' she snapped. 'I'm not going to do anything else to hurt you.'

Marc turned and looked at her with amusement.

'I don't believe you could hurt me,' he said. 'And where are you off to now? If you're planning to run off somewhere and sob your heart out, I forbid it.'

Jane gave a choking laugh.

'What would you care?' she exclaimed unsteadily. 'Anyway, as it happens, I'm just going to bed.'

'I'll come and prepare a guest-room for you,' offered Marc.

'No, you won't!' she shouted. 'I'm not a guest. I live here! I've got a perfectly good room of my own upstairs.'

'Ah, of course,' murmured Marc with dawning comprehension. 'The locked room that Monsieur West told me he had left his possessions in. The one opposite the head of the stairs?'

'Yes, and I might as well warn you right now that I'm not just staying there tonight. I'm staying as long as I like. I won't move out just to please you and I don't care what kind of legal contract you've got. If you want me to go then you'll have to drag me out of here.'

Marc's smile broadened.

'That too might be interesting,' he said softly.

Jane made a strangled sound deep in the back of her throat.

'You're impossible!'

Her rage boiled over. She stepped out into the hall and slammed the door, then she remembered his earlier taunt that she had no manners. With a contemptuous snort she swung round and reopened it. She poked her head back into the sitting-room.

'Thanks for the meal!' she hissed. Then she withdrew and slammed the door so hard that the grandfather clock struck twice in protest.

Upstairs, Jane was in no way soothed by the familiar green-sprigged wallpaper, lace curtains and soft lighting of her bedroom. On the contrary, she was doubly annoyed to find that her father really had left a lot of his belongings in her room. Sweeping a pile of cardboard cartons off her bed so that they landed on the floor with ominous crashes, she crawled under the feather duvet, snapped off the bedside lamp and closed her eyes. Her heart was still thudding angrily from her encounter with Marc and she felt like a racing car running on high octane fuel. She intended to stay awake trying to think out some plan of action to protect her vineyard and her home, but soon exhaustion took over and she fell asleep.

Not that this was in any way a refreshing experience. Her dreams were troubled by the roaring of plane engines, the shattering of bottles and confused

visions of Marc Le Rossignol prowling in the firelight
like a demon king. Towards dawn these restless nightmares gave way to a deep, annihilating slumber in
which she was conscious of cool, fresh country air
rippling the curtains and of branches tapping softly
against her window. It was almost noon when at last
she woke up properly. For a moment she had a
tranquil sense of wellbeing, which was even accompanied by an odd sense of exhilaration. Then the
memories of the previous night came hurtling back
to her and she gave a sudden groan.

'Oh, no! He can't take this place away from me.
He can't! He can't!'

Jumping out of bed, she ran to the window and
flung open the curtains. The Japanese maple which
had been tapping out its Morse code all through her
dreams waved a vivid canopy of scarlet leaves against
a bright blue sky. Raising the sash window even
higher, she leaned on the windowsill and looked out.
In spite of her worries, the scene still made her heart
lift. Down below was the vivid green of the garden
contained within a darker green yew hedge. Beyond
that were the rows and rows of lime-green grapevines,
rustling peacefully in the autumn sunshine. In the distance the hills looked dark blue against the paler blue
of the sky. It seemed a double irony that disaster
should threaten her on such a beautiful day. Well, she
wasn't going to give up without a fight!

Luckily her room had a tiny *en suite* bathroom with
a shower, so she didn't have to face Marc while she
was still tousled and yawning. After a long reviving
shower she dressed in clean jeans, a shirt and
espadrilles, tied her unruly hair back in a riotous
ponytail and went downstairs. She was in the kitchen

burning her second lot of toast when Marc suddenly
appeared. He snatched the smoking toast, swore softly
in French as it burned his fingers, and dropped it into
the bin. A moment later he unplugged the toaster and
dropped that in on top of the burnt bread.

'What are you doing?' cried Jane indignantly.
'We've had that toaster for fifteen years.'

'That is obvious,' retorted Marc. 'It's bad enough
when somebody efficient like me makes the toast. But
you, you don't even watch it and your sense of smell
evidently doesn't work. Do you want to burn the
whole house down? And don't worry about the
toaster. I'll buy you another one tomorrow.'

'I don't want another toaster!' cried Jane. 'I want
that one.'

Even to her own ears she sounded remarkably like
a petulant six-year-old. It was even worse when she
ran to the bin and tried to snatch the toaster back out.
Marc barred her way.

'You wish to fight me for it?' he invited.

Jane ground her teeth.

'No.'

'Ah, *bon*. You have some sense after all. I had
begun to wonder. And, since that is the last slice of
bread you have just burnt, perhaps you will join me
in a decent breakfast.'

'What do you mean "a decent breakfast"?' asked
Jane suspiciously.

'Coffee—real coffee—almond croissants, a ba-
guette. There are some surprisingly good bakeries in
Tasmania.'

Jane scowled silently. She wanted to refuse, but the
pastries which Marc was laying out in a basket on the
kitchen table looked far too delectable to resist. Those

yummy little crescents filled with almond paste, dusted with flaked almonds and icing sugar—surely it wouldn't hurt if she had just one of them? After all, there was no point in starving even if her whole life was in ruins.

'All right,' she agreed ungraciously.

Fortified by two cups of fragrant black coffee, an almond croissant, a *pain au chocolat* and a large piece of crusty French bread, Jane was beginning to feel that Marc might not be quite such a monster as she had thought the previous evening. The way his gaze rested on her in that quiet, mocking scrutiny still unnerved her, but perhaps underneath he was really quite nice. She didn't know that her opinion would change before the morning was over.

'Well,' said Marc, when they had finally rinsed the dirty plates and cups and put them in the dishwasher. 'I think it's time we phoned your father.'

'All right,' agreed Jane with lead in her heart.

It was every bit as bad as she had feared. The telephone number which Marc gave her proved to be in Queenstown in New Zealand. When she first came on the line her father proclaimed himself delighted to hear her, but as soon as he realised she was back in Australia and had learnt about Marc's contract on the vineyard his manner changed. He became defensive and began to bluster. First he told Jane that he had signed the contract for her own good because Marc's offer had been too handsome to refuse and assured her that they would both make a mint of money out of a set of time-share apartments he was planning to build.

Jane tried to reason with him, then pleaded, and finally lost her temper and began to shout. At that point Marc seized the telephone and took over. Where Jane had been impassioned and incoherent, he was cool and rational, but Jane had the impression that his cool questioning was beginning to wear her father down. It was tantalising to listen to a one-sided conversation, but a wild hope rose in her as she realised that Marc was getting the better of her father on every point. It was all the more of a disappointment when Marc uttered a pleasant farewell without obtaining any clear resolution of the problem.

'What happened?' cried Jane hotly. 'You had him on the run! You could have made him back out of the whole deal, couldn't you?'

Marc shrugged.

'Probably.'

'Then why didn't you?' she demanded. 'The whole situation is completely unfair to me—you told him that yourself! So why didn't you make him give up?'

'Because I chose not to,' he replied.

Jane's disappointment was so acute that she felt like shouting or hitting something. Preferably Marc. Somehow over breakfast she had begun to think of him not so much as an unwanted invader but as her protector and ally. Now she realised bitterly that he was only interested in protecting his own interests.

'I suppose that's fair enough,' she sneered. 'Naturally you're only interested in your own interests. Why should I expect anything else?'

Marc's pupils narrowed to tiny, opaque points of light that seemed for an instant to glitter dangerously. Then he gave her a long, appraising look.

'Never mind my reasons. The important thing is that I'm staying here for the full three months. The question now is, What's going to happen to you?'

'I'm staying here too,' insisted Jane. 'I'm not moving.'

Marc's lips twisted into an odd smile.

'And when the irresistible meets the immovable, what happens?'

'I wouldn't call you irresistible,' said Jane scathingly.

'And I wouldn't call you immovable,' he murmured. His voice was husky and his eyes held a suave, mocking glint that seemed to conceal something brooding and wild beneath it. He reminded Jane of a tiger on a leash. 'I feel sure I could move you if I tried.'

'Stop playing games!' she cried. 'I'm staying here and that's that.'

'Really? And what will you do for money? I suppose your father has left you adequately provided for?'

Jane stared at him, aghast. Supposing he hadn't? She and her father had a joint account which had served both for housekeeping and the expenses of the property. Either of them could withdraw money at any time and she had never fussed about it too much, even though her mother had warned her that it was unwise. Now a tremor of misgiving went through her. What if her father had cleaned the account out?

'I'm sure he's left me enough money!' she cried, leaping instantly to her father's defence.

With a sceptical expression Marc picked up the phone again and held it out to her.

'Why don't you phone your bank manager and check?'

Jane's fingers were shaking as she punched in the numbers. She wished Marc wouldn't keep looking at

her with that half pitying, half contemptuous stare.
Her heart beat more and more frantically and, when
at last she got her bank manager on the line, her questions came out in a breathless staccato rush. Even
before he answered her something in the quality of
his long, initial silence told her that she was in for a
bitter disappointment. Waves of humiliation and
anger washed over her as she set down the phone
again.

'Well? Has he left you enough money?'

'No,' she flared. 'You knew he wouldn't, didn't
you? He's transferred everything to New Zealand
except for a few dollars. What am I going to do? There
are Charlie's wages to be paid and soon there'll be
grape-pickers for the harvest.'

'Don't work yourself into a state,' advised Marc
coolly. 'Those things are my concern now. Under the
terms of the contract I signed, I'm responsible for all
the expenses to do with the vineyard for the next three
months. The real difficulty is you. It seems you're
thrown on my charity, Jane. If I choose to show any.'

She stared at him in horror as the implication of
his words sank in. If she stayed here then every
mouthful she ate, every bar of soap she washed her
hands with would be paid for by Marc Le Rossignol!
And the taunting smile that touched the corners of
his mouth showed that he was thinking exactly the
same thought.

'Yes, *chérie*, I'm afraid so. If you stay here you will
have to come down every morning and beg me sweetly
to share my croissants with you. You'll have to ask
me for money to go shopping or to buy petrol for the
car. Is that what you want?'

'Oh, go to hell!' flared Jane.

Marc laughed, in no way upset by her spurt of temper.

'I've always thought my ideal woman would be tall, red-haired and gracious in any situation,' he remarked. 'But you, you remind me of... What's that ferocious little creature you have here? The one that snarls and bares its teeth? A devil, that's it. You're a little Tasmanian devil, aren't you?'

Jane gave him a long, smouldering, silent glare.

'They're very bad-tempered creatures,' continued Marc in a conversational tone. 'Although I'm told they make good pets if you can tame them—but only one man in a thousand is capable of doing it.'

'Just try!' snapped Jane.

Marc smiled provocatively.

'I might. It would be a challenge to see if I could get you eating out of my hand. All right, enough of these games! What's to become of you?'

'I'm staying here,' insisted Jane.

'What about when you want to go to the shops, or to buy petrol, or clothes, or to visit the hairdresser's?'

'I never go to the hairdresser's!'

'Never?' marvelled Marc. 'You mean all that long, blonde, wonderful hair is natural?'

'Yes.'

'It's very beautiful,' said Marc, momentarily diverted. 'But we must not lose the thread of our conversation. Even if you don't go to the hairdresser's, there must be some place where you need to spend money.'

'I won't go out at all,' threatened Jane. 'I'll just stay here at the house until you leave.'

Marc's lips twitched. 'And if I choose not to feed you?'

'I'll eat grapes.'

'*Quelle drôle de femme! Comme elle est farouche!* No, no, Jane, this won't do. In any case, I need all the grapes I can get to make the best possible wine here. I have a much more sensible idea. I'll employ you.'

'Employ me?' echoed Jane in a baffled tone.

'Yes, you can be my personal assistant for the next three months on a salary of——' He named a figure which made Jane blink at its generosity.

'Why?' she asked suspiciously. 'Why would you want to do a thing like that?'

Marc shrugged.

'It seems a very good idea. You could learn a lot from me, Jane. I'm thirty-four years old; I've been a professional winemaker for the last twelve years and I've been working in my family vineyard for even longer than that. It's an excellent opportunity for you.'

'Maybe,' admitted Jane grudgingly. 'But what's in it for you?'

'Well, I don't want you starving on the streets or plotting sabotage behind my back. This way I can keep an eye on you. Besides, I'd like to try my skills at taming a genuine Tasmanian devil.'

Jane hated being teased. Ever since childhood it had been the surest way to make her fly into a rage. Now she opened her mouth to protest hotly, to refuse Marc's stupid, insulting proposition, and then paused. If she didn't accept, what could she do? She would either have to leave the place entirely or stay here on even more humiliating terms. Was she really prepared to beg for croissants every morning? No way! Wasn't it better to be Marc's employee? Besides, if she stayed then she might be able to talk him out of buying the property at all...

A sweet radiant smile replaced her scowl.

'All right,' she agreed meekly. 'It's a deal.'

Marc suddenly looked uneasy.

'There are conditions,' he warned. 'No bombs in the car, no fires in the equipment shed, no poison in the coffee.'

'*Moi*?' demanded Jane innocently.

Marc sighed and shook his head.

'For centuries the men of my family have had the gift of prophecy,' he lamented. 'They are forewarned of disaster to the Le Rossignols by a mysterious prickle down their spines. Me, I have a mysterious prickle down my spine.'

In spite of Marc's foreboding no disasters happened immediately. As a matter of fact he and Jane soon developed a strong professional respect for each other. Yet, much as she admired Marc's knowledge about vineyards, Jane found the whole situation fraught with unbearable tension. In her rash determination to hold on to her territory at any cost, she had not stopped to consider what an intimate situation she was being plunged into with this suave, mocking Frenchman.

Morning after morning she came downstairs and had to look at him over the breakfast table, just as if they were married. There were so many decisions to be made about what they would eat for dinner, whose turn it was to load the washing machine, whether or not friends should be invited over for Sunday lunch. Worst of all was the alarming and wholly unwelcome attraction that she felt towards him. Even though she tried to fight against it, Jane

was no more immune to Marc's smouldering animal
magnetism than any other woman would have been.
Her weakness infuriated her. She had never trusted
men with those brooding, bedroom eyes or that
hoarse, caressing voice. At any rate not since she was
nineteen years old and had fallen violently in love with
Michael Barrett, her chemistry tutor in Adelaide.

Michael had pursued her with an ardour that had
flattered and excited her and she had been bitterly dis-
illusioned to overhear other students joking crudely
about the way he always tried to seduce the prettiest
girl in each new class. Fortunately matters had not
gone quite that far between them although they had
gone quite far enough to lacerate Jane's pride. Her
cheeks burned even now whenever she thought of one
particularly torrid evening in Michael's flat when he
had kissed her violently and—— Well, she felt bitterly
certain that Marc was another man just like that.
Someone only interested in scoring women as if they
were goals in a soccer match, and Jane had no intention of adding to his tally!

All the same, it became harder and harder to face
him calmly over the breakfast table each morning,
particularly since he was in the habit of appearing in
a navy-blue towelling dressing-gown that left the top
of his muscular, tanned chest exposed. Again and
again Jane felt her eyes straying in horrified fasci-
nation to the dark, springy hairs that curled over the
V of fabric, then up the brown column of his neck
to the aggressive line of his jaw and the taunting half-
smile that always seemed to hover around his lips as
he read the newspaper. What a fool she was! Why
couldn't she just settle for someone dull and nice and
devoted like Brett? The restless yearning she felt for

a man who would make her blood pulse like molten fire through her veins was probably quite insane! It seemed to be a law of nature that the only men who made her heart pound and her breath come faster were utterly worthless like Michael. Or dangerous and probably untrustworthy like Marc. No, she would be much wiser to give up crying for the moon and settle for second best.

When her twenty-seventh birthday arrived two weeks after her return from France, she was so depressed that she almost made up her mind to do exactly that. Over breakfast she sat gloomily stirring her coffee and sighing quietly to herself. If she knew Brett, he was bound to arrive some time during the day, probably with a bale of wire for the vineyard and definitely with another one of his matter of fact proposals. Well, this time she really ought to accept! After all, she wanted a home and children and she was fond of Brett. Besides, she wasn't getting any younger and she didn't want to feel as if love had passed her by completely. Sometimes she thought she was probably the only twenty-seven-year-old virgin in Australia. Or even in the world. She sighed again.

'*Mon Dieu*!' exclaimed Marc. 'What is the matter with you? Do you have asthma?'

'No,' retorted Jane with a scowl. She rose to her feet abruptly, pushing away her coffee-cup, and headed for the French doors which led out of the kitchen into the garden.

'Where are you going?' demanded Marc with a frown.

Jane paused with her hand on the door handle and turned back to look at him. An unwanted thrill of excitement tingled through her as she scanned every detail of his body from his carelessly brushed-back hair, his narrowed eyes and twisted smile to his lean, muscular body which seemed to strain against the confining dressing-gown. She shuddered and looked away.

'Into the garden,' she replied drily and then chanted half to herself, 'Nobody loves me, everybody hates me, I'm going into the garden to eat worms!'

The baffled look on Marc's face almost made her laugh as she escaped into the cool, dewy crispness of the garden. Luckily the fine autumn weather was holding well. Although there was an early morning freshness in the air, the cloudless blue sky held the promise of a fine day. If the good weather held she should soon have an excellent harvest.

Yet the lift in her spirits was only momentary and before long she was pacing around the shrubs and flowerbeds feeling tragic again. What a mess everything was! It looked as if she was going to lose her home and her livelihood; nobody *did* love her except Brett and she really wished he wouldn't and, worst of all, she was locked into this ridiculous, humiliating situation with Marc Le Rossignol, whom she both desired and disliked, with equal fervour!

She was on her third circuit of the garden when she heard the sound of a utility truck pulling up in the turning circle behind the house. Her spirits plummeted even further. It had to be Brett! Feeling as if she were about to make a visit to the dentist, Jane sat down at the pine table near the barbecue. If he asks me to marry him, I'll say yes, she told herself defiantly. At least it will make Brett happy and it will get Marc Le Rossignol out of my life forever!

A moment later Brett came strolling around the corner of the house with a lettuce under his arm.

'Happy birthday,' he said.

'Thanks, Brett.'

'I've got some irrigation pipe out in the ute for you. I thought you'd prefer something practical.'

'Thanks. That's very nice of you.'

'No worries. And I thought you could do with a lettuce from my veggie garden.'

He set the lettuce down on the table in front of her and then took Jane in his arms as she rose to her feet. His face looked as red and good-natured as ever and she wanted to return the fervent emotion that she saw shining in his eyes, but somehow she couldn't. At the last moment, as he bent to kiss her, she turned her head so that his kiss landed on her cheek instead of her lips.

'Ah, come on, Jane,' he protested. 'You can do better than that. Give us a proper kiss.'

Jane's instinct was to run, but she steeled herself to obey. Glancing at the kitchen, she saw that Marc was standing just inside the French doors and suddenly a crazy impulse seized her to tell Brett that it was Marc she loved and to flee inside to him. How stupid could she be? Instead she flung her arms around Brett's waist and kissed him warmly on the lips. Brett looked shocked and then delighted. He kissed her back with a warm, moist fervour that made her stiffen with distaste.

'Ah, that's the way,' he exclaimed, approvingly at last. 'I knew you'd come round if I waited long enough! Listen, Jane, what do you say we stop all this pussyfooting around and get married right away?'

Jane stared at him in horror. This was the proposal she had been waiting for—the proposal she had meant to accept. She opened her mouth to say yes and was seized by such a blind, unreasoning panic that for a moment she could say nothing at all.

'No!' she wailed at last, pushing away the bewildered farmer. 'I'm sorry, Brett, you're a really, really nice man, but I don't love you and I never will. Now please go away!'

Hurtling into the house, she almost knocked Marc down in her mad rush.

'Get out of my way!' she cried impatiently, confusingly aware of his strong hands steadying her arms, the spicy, masculine scent of his body so close to hers, the questioning glint in his eyes. The irrelevant thought occurred to her that she would have no trouble kissing Marc or agreeing to marry him. She gave him a violent push and ran for the stairs.

'Don't let him follow me!' she begged over her shoulder, and then vanished.

Much as she simply wanted to race up the stairs two at a time, lock herself in her wardrobe and never come out again, Jane couldn't help pausing anxiously on the stairs to see what happened. A moment later she heard Brett's heavy tread as he entered the kitchen.

'Get out of my way, mate,' he ordered, amiably enough.

Craning her neck, Jane risked a look, and saw that Marc was barring Brett's way with equal amiability.

'She doesn't want to see you,' said Marc, in a pleasant voice that held an undertone of steel.

'Now, look here,' protested Brett. 'I'm not just mucking about and leading her on, you know. I came here to ask Jane to marry me.'

'I'm sorry for you. But it seems you have your answer and the answer is no.'

'This is your fault,' said Brett accusingly. 'Coming here, filling her head with your fancy foreign ideas. I'll bet you're just trying to turn her against me so that you can have some rotten little affair with her and then go off and leave her broken-hearted.'

'Whatever happens between Jane and me is none of your business,' replied Marc with aristocratic hauteur. 'But, since you seem a decent fellow, I will tell you this. In fact, Jane and I have an understanding between us. Naturally in these circumstances she does not want to be involved with any other man. Nor would I permit it.'

'But you've only been staying here with her for two flaming weeks!' exclaimed Brett in an outraged voice. 'How the hell can you have an understanding with her in that time?'

'You seem to forget that she was in France for six months before that,' Marc reminded him.

Brett's face creased into a baffled frown.

'You mean, you knew her in France before you came here?' he demanded.

With the merest upward flick of his eyebrows, Marc contrived to suggest that this was so.

'Well, she never said anything to me about it!' insisted Brett belligerently.

'Why should she tell you?' countered Marc. 'She regards you as a dear friend, certainly, but she would hardly want to discuss her love for another man with you.'

'Oh, yeah, love is it?' demanded Brett sceptically. 'Well, it had better be, mate, and the real thing into the bargain. Because I'll tell you this. I'm not going to quarrel with any other bloke if he wins Jane fair and square and she really prefers him to me. But if you're taking advantage of her and your intentions aren't serious, I'll knock your flaming teeth down your throat!'

'Would I be thinking of buying this property if my intentions weren't serious?' asked Marc coolly. 'Now, come on, Brett, Jane has asked you to leave. Please go quietly and we can all meet one day soon for a drink as friends.'

'All right,' grumbled Brett. 'But you watch yourself, mate, because I'll have my eye on you, see?'

The moment Jane heard the utility truck departing, she came slowly down the stairs and appeared in the kitchen with a shamefaced expression. Her emotions were in turmoil. She felt shocked and guilty at precipitating the whole scene by her recklessness in kissing Brett. At the same time she was both grateful to Marc for getting rid of him and appalled and embarrassed by the lies and half-truths he had told to do so. It made her feel even more troubled to see that Marc looked as cool and unruffled as ever.

'What was that all about?' he demanded with an odd expression.

Jane winced.

'Don't ask!' she begged, pulling a face. 'The whole situation was so awful I could just die!'

'You seem to me to have a very frivolous and unreliable character,' said Marc disapprovingly. 'One minute you're kissing that poor young man violently, if very ineptly, the next you're ordering him to leave the premises and asking me to get rid of him. If I'm going to act like a bouncer in a nightclub, at least I want to know what's going on here.'

'Oh, you wouldn't understand!' burst out Jane unhappily. 'You see, it's my birthday and I knew Brett would ask me to marry him—he always does. Only this time I was going to say yes, but then he gave me the lettuce and then I kissed him and then I said no and so he followed me inside.'

'Ah, that explains everything,' murmured Marc with a glint of amusement in his eyes.

'Don't laugh at me!' shouted Jane hotly. 'This is serious!'

'Serious, *ma foi*! Of course it is serious. A proposal of marriage is always serious. But you have not told me the most important thing. When this excellent young man came to propose to you with a lettuce— why a lettuce, I ask myself? Why not a bunch of roses?—why did you say no?'

'Because I don't love him,' wailed Jane. 'And I thought I could go through with it, but I couldn't.'

'Ah, so this is why you kissed him with your eyes closed and your face screwed up as if you were taking the medicine?'

'You were watching!' protested Jane indignantly.

'I couldn't help it. I was so close to the French doors that it happened before I could move away. You looked ridiculous, both of you. As a kiss, it was not impressive.'

'Oh, really?' demanded Jane. 'I suppose you could do much better?'

'Of course.'

Before she knew what was happening, Marc swept her into his arms with a force that made a surprised gasp burst from her lips. It was the last sound she made for a considerable time.

Scarcely able to breathe in that crushing embrace, she felt his warm mouth come down on hers and found herself being kissed with a passion that made her dizzy. A high-voltage current seemed to tingle through every part of her body and her resistance crumbled. She melted into Marc's arms and lifted her trembling lips to his as his hold tightened further. Her eyes closed and she let herself float on a tide of sensual arousal so urgent that it shocked her. Never before had she experienced such intense desire. A dark, throbbing heat seemed to be spreading through every part of her so that she felt powerless to resist as Marc's mouth plundered hers. Her nipples rose into hard, tight buds and her heart began to hammer frantically, making every pulse in her body leap. A riot of sensations clamoured for her attention. She felt acutely conscious of the powerful, insistent pressure of Marc's virile body against hers, of the rhythmic, demanding caress of his hands moving down her spine, of the heady, intoxicating masculine smell that rose from his body in waves. All she wanted in that moment of wildness was to fling off the clothes that constrained her and offer herself to him passionately and completely. But when his hands came up and cupped her tingling breasts, she broke away with a muffled gasp.

'Don't, Marc!'

He put his thumb under her chin and tilted her face, scanning it with smouldering brown eyes.

'I thought you wanted me,' he murmured hoarsely.

She was too far gone for anything but complete honesty.

'I did . . . I do. But——'

She broke off and a hot flush of shame burned in her cheeks.

'But you're a nice girl who doesn't play games with men she hardly knows,' he finished for her.

Games? Was that all it had meant to him, that kiss which had inflamed her, igniting all kinds of unfamiliar passions within her?

'That's right,' she said coldly and wrenched away from him.

He caught her by the arm.

'Did you know that you have the most enchanting green eyes I have ever seen?' he asked.

'Oh, really? Is that why you kissed me? Because of my enchanting green eyes?'

'Exactly,' he agreed in an amused voice.

Darting a swift, angry glance at him she saw that he could not possibly have been as stirred by that encounter as she had been. Oh, he was aroused by her, she did not doubt that. The narrowing of his eyes, the tension in his muscles, the hard, hot, ruthless pressure of his body had told her that. But his feelings were not involved. The smug, nonchalant self-possession with which Marc Le Rossignol confronted the world was quite untouched. A feeling of vengeful rage rose in Jane's throat, threatening to choke her. She wanted to hit out, hurt him, make him vulnerable the way lesser human beings were.

'I hate you,' she breathed. 'I wish you'd never come here.'

'So, what are you going to do about it?' he taunted.

CHAPTER THREE

'I'LL do anything I can to make you leave,' vowed Jane.

'Does that include dirty tricks?' demanded Marc with a lift of his eyebrows.

'I said anything!' she retorted.

Then, giving him another long, burning look over her shoulder, she crossed the room to the French doors. Marc reached her just as she gripped the handle and whirled her around to face him.

'Are you going out to eat worms again?' he demanded mockingly. 'I've got a better idea. Why don't you have lunch with me today?'

'I've just had breakfast,' she pointed out.

He shrugged, in no way perturbed by her obvious hostility.

'I mean later in the day, naturally. It's time we got to know each other.'

'No, thanks.'

His mouth hardened.

'Consider it an order,' he said. 'It's part of your job to brief me on the vineyard. You can do it while we talk over lunch.'

Jane scowled, but Marc remained cool and unruffled by her annoyance, merely watching her with a faint, sardonic lift of his eyebrows.

'All right,' she agreed at last.

'Is there anywhere special you'd like to go?' asked Marc, flashing her a triumphant smile.

For a moment she was tempted to take him to a particularly unsavoury backstreet dive where she had once eaten the most revolting hamburger in her life with Brett. Forever afterwards she had called the place the Greasy Spoon, but childish tactics of that kind were only likely to irritate Marc without achieving anything.

'We could go to Moorilla Winery,' she suggested slowly. 'That's a family vineyard like the one I'm trying to establish here. It's just outside of Hobart on the banks of the Derwent River and it has a very pleasant restaurant. You might like to try some of their wines.'

'That's a good idea,' agreed Marc approvingly.

Shortly after one o'clock they drove up the Moorilla estate's winding driveway which led out along a spit of land at Claremont. The autumn sun was still shining tranquilly, gilding the neat rows of green vines, sparkling off the blue waters of the river and warming the terracotta tiles at the entrance to the restaurant. Seeing the tables set invitingly on the balcony, Marc turned to Jane with a questioning look.

'Why don't we eat outside, seeing the weather is so fine?' he suggested.

'Just as you like,' replied Jane. 'But don't expect the weather to stay like this for long, will you? It's always very changeable here. We get gales, bushfires, cold weather, rain. There are lots of things that could ruin your grape harvest.'

Marc smiled lazily.

'If I didn't know better I'd say that you were trying to turn me off this place, but I've done my homework. I know that a lot of what you're saying is true. Tasmanian summers *are* colder on average than those in France. I also know that some very fine wine is being made here at Moorilla and I intend to sample some of it right now. So why don't you stop telling me atrocity stories and join me?'

The words were spoken pleasantly enough, but they were obviously more in the nature of a command than an invitation. Seething inwardly, Jane was forced to obey. Yet the ordeal was more pleasant than she had anticipated. Once the waiter had been informed of Marc's interest and background he brought an array of wines on a tray for them to sample. In spite of her resentment towards Marc, Jane soon became absorbed in tasting, comparing and discussing. After they had tried three white wines and two reds, she belatedly realised that she was starving.

'Don't you want to eat?' she demanded.

'What would you suggest?' asked Marc, picking up a menu.

'I think you ought to try a mixed platter of local delicacies and perhaps have some seafood or steak to follow.'

Before long they were each supplied with a plate of smoked beef, baby quail, fresh oysters and other tempting hors-d'oeuvres.

'This food is excellent,' exclaimed Marc with obvious surprise.

Jane felt a momentary pleasure which she sternly quelled. She had always been proud of the island where she lived and enjoyed introducing strangers to its fine food, but she didn't want Marc to start liking the place too much. Nor did she intend to let down her guard enough to start liking him.

'Well, Tasmanian food is good,' she admitted in an offhand tone. 'But I don't think you'd like living here.

It's right at the end of the world, so far away from everything you've grown up with. You'd miss the buildings and the culture and the traditions of France.'

A faint smile flickered around the edges of Marc's mouth.

'I won't need to miss them,' he pointed out. 'You seem to forget that my plan is to have the best of both worlds. Europe for tradition and cosmopolitan sophistication, this island for the great escape. Bordeaux for half the year, Tasmania for the rest. What could be better?'

'You actually live in Bordeaux?' asked Jane, her hostility momentarily forgotten.

'Yes, have you been there?'

She nodded as she swallowed a chilled oyster.

'Mmm. It's a beautiful area.'

'Very beautiful,' agreed Marc in a matter-of-fact tone. 'I can never decide when it's most beautiful. In the summer with the vines lush and green and a heat-haze shimmering up from the earth. Or in autumn, when we have our harvest and the big parties to follow the picking. Or in springtime when there are hidden wildflowers out in the woods. Or even in the winter when the whole place is stark and cold with dormant vines like black brush strokes against the white snow.'

Jane gave him a troubled look, feeling unwillingly touched by the warmth in his voice as he spoke of his homeland. For a moment he sounded quite sensitive, as if he really cared about the place. Then she felt an immediate reaction of scorn. Marc Le Rossignol sensitive? Never! He was about as sensitive as a length of irrigation pipe. All the same, his mention of Bordeaux intrigued her. Hadn't he said something earlier on about having a family vineyard there?

'Didn't you tell me that your family had been making wine there for five hundred years?' she demanded.

'Yes,' agreed Marc.

Five hundred years! It gave her goose-bumps just to think of it.

'How wonderful to have a family tradition like that! But what's the vineyard like?' she asked curiously. 'What's your family like? Tell me about it all.'

Marc shrugged.

'The equipment is old and often rather shabby. So is the house, actually. Our home is just outside the village of St Sulpice. And let me tell you that if tradition is what you like then you'd be in ecstasies in Bordeaux. It seems to me that the hand of tradition lies heavy on everything we do there. Sometimes that's marvellous. Everyone in the village knows you and you know them and there are little rituals about anything you do, even if it's just pruning vines or drinking coffee in a pavement café. In some ways that's good, but at other times I've felt as if tradition was like a weight, crushing me down.'

'What do you mean?'

'I'll give you an example,' offered Marc, his eyes kindling as if he were going into battle. 'Some of the grapes in our vineyard were old varieties which were hard to pick and were only ever used for making a very undistinguished *vin ordinaire*. That always annoyed me, so in the end I took matters into my own hands. I brought in earthmovers, razed the vines to the ground, used mustard gas to fumigate the earth. Then I planted new varieties. *Mon Dieu*! You should have heard the outcry. Anyone would have thought it was the villagers that I had gassed. Everyone was up in arms—my old friends, even my family—all abusing me and complaining about my violent destructive nature. I can still see my father in his shabby old overalls and cap with tears in his eyes as he told me how I had brought shame on all the family of Le Rossignol.'

Jane smiled at the image. Obviously Marc came from quite a humble background, in spite of his aristocratic manner. Somehow the realisation made her thaw a little towards him, particularly since there was an unmistakable note of affection beneath his annoyance as he spoke of his family. Her face shadowed as she thought of her own unreliable father and her distinctly unmaternal mother.

'You're very fond of your family, aren't you?' she asked with a touch of envy.

'Of course I'm very fond of them,' agreed Marc wearily. 'But they're like all families. I love them and they drive me mad. Every last one of them.'

Jane blinked.

'How many of them are there?' she asked.

'Well, there's my father—he's retired but he still keeps a finger in the wine vat—and my mother, whose main interests in life are the kitchen, the garden and the grandchildren. Two younger brothers—Paul and Robert—both married, both proper *traditional* winemakers, and a younger sister Laurette, who is a research chemist. You'd like Laurette; she's lived in the United States and she's open-minded, but even she has now become engaged to a *traditional* winemaker. And then there is me. The rebel, the troublemaker, the destroyer of ancient hallowed vines. "A good thing he went to Australia!" my dear relatives say to each other with a shudder of relief. ''Perhaps our vine-yards will be spared any further destruction!'' '

Jane's eyes twinkled in spite of herself.

'Just as a matter of interest,' she asked, 'how did those new vines that you planted turn out?'

Marc grinned.

'They did very well. We got three times the yield of the old vines and they were much easier to pick. That's the biggest reason my family has never for-given me.'

'I suppose they're still fond of you though, aren't they?' she said in a wistful voice.

'Of course. But you say that in an odd tone. Perhaps you fear that your family is not fond of you?'

She was alarmed by his perception and felt herself shrinking like a sea anemone at the touch of a probing hand.

'I haven't much family,' she replied with a shrug. 'Only my father and my mother.'

'A father who tries to sell the property behind your back,' murmured Marc thoughtfully. 'What about your mother? Is she still alive?'

Jane swallowed, dropped her eyes and drew a pattern on the rim of her wine glass with her finger.

'Yes,' she agreed, 'but she's hardly what you'd call the motherly type.'

'No brothers, no sisters?' quizzed Marc.

'No. My parents didn't really hit if off. They got divorced when I was ten years old. Before that my mother had been an architect in Melbourne so after they split up she went off with a huge sigh of relief to resume her career.'

'And you went with her, naturally?'

'No,' replied Jane. 'She didn't want me. Oh, she said it was because I loved the farm so much that she couldn't bear to take me away from it, but I would have gone like a shot to be with her. The real reason was that she just plain didn't want me. After the divorce I went to a boarding-school and spent most of my holidays with my father.'

Even now at twenty-seven she couldn't quite keep the pain out of her voice. Why am I telling him this? she thought savagely. I've never mentioned it to anyone before. She was horrified when he suddenly reached out and gripped her free hand.

'*Pauvre petite*,' he murmured.

'No,' she said through her teeth. 'I'm not a poor little thing! I'm tough and unscrupulous and you'd better not forget it.'

At that moment they were interrupted by the arrival of their main course. Throughout the rest of the meal Jane was conscious of Marc's lazy scrutiny, and she found it hard to keep her mind on the conversation. All the time that they were talking about rainfall and grape varieties her thoughts kept drifting to the way he had kissed her that morning, and to that fragment of discussion about their respective families.

She wished she hadn't told him all that sentimental guff about her mother, just as if she had been a pathetic Little Orphan Annie abandoned in a laundry basket on somebody's doorstep! It sounded uncomfortably like self-pity and it also filled her with a superstitious fear that if Marc knew the nature of her deepest insecurities, it would give him power over her.

Jane liked people to think that she was tough and self-reliant and resourceful, not as soft as marshmallow. Of course the real truth was that she was a seething mass of contradictions. By nature she had always been trusting and impetuous, open about her feelings and with a quick temper, but the nagging fear that neither of her parents really loved her or wanted her had always been too private and secret to reveal to anyone until now. So why had she told Marc? Perhaps because he had an uncanny knack of getting under her skin and making her blurt out things she really didn't want to say.

It was doubly annoying since he was so self-possessed and inscrutable himself. Weren't Frenchmen supposed to be hot-blooded and passionate and volatile? Well, not this one! He had all the controlled power of a dormant volcano and only the occasional spurt of anger or desire gave any hint of the molten depths that might lurk beneath his tranquil exterior. She remembered his narrowed, smouldering eyes as he kissed her and a secret conviction rose inside her that in the right circumstances Marc Le Rossignol might blaze completely out of control. Suddenly she felt a tempestuous urge to provoke him, to make him lose his nonchalance and boil over with…with what? Passion, rage, jealousy? But how could she ever arouse such feelings in him? And why should she even want to?

She realised that Marc had stopped talking about vineyards and was applying himself to the serious business of sipping his wine and enjoying his beefsteak. His absorption gave Jane the opportunity to study him at her leisure. She looked again at his chiselled features, with the rugged jaw and twisted smile, and let her gaze travel down over his Pierre Cardin shirt to the brown, capable hands resting on the table.

There was a strange intimacy about watching the dark hairs that straggled from beneath his Rolex watch, the long, tapered fingers that looked both strong and sensitive.

I wonder what he'd be like in bed? thought Jane, and then blushed hotly with shock and a furtive thrill of excitement at the unfamiliar sensual images that immediately filled her head. What was wrong with her? Never in her life had she sat looking at a man and imagining such appalling and delicious things. I'd like to unbutton his shirt slowly, she thought, and slip my hands inside and feel that warm, hard muscular chest with the rough hair on it. Or even touch his nipples and tease them with my fingertips, and then let my fingers stray down to his belt ... I'd unbuckle it and slip my hands inside and feel him grow hot and hard under my touch. Or... I know! I'd like to be in bed with him, both of us naked, and I'd cover him with fruit. Strawberries and whipped cream from the navel down and I'd nibble it and lick it off slowly, going lower and lower each time, until... She swallowed hard and closed her eyes for an instant with a faint sigh. Or I'd like to be in a rainforest with him. A warm, steamy jungly rainforest, with no mosquitoes but a glorious, crystal-clear pool and a waterfall splashing into it. We'd take off our clothes and swim, then I'd be standing under the waterfall and he'd suddenly creep up on me and pounce. He'd swing me round and kiss me just the way he did this morning and...

'What appeals to you most?' asked Marc, in a smoky, caressing voice.

Jane sat up with a jerk and stared at him in horror. Had he read her mind? Then she realised that the

waitress had returned to remove their empty plates
and was now proffering two dessert menus. The wild
rose colour in her cheeks slowly subsided and she
muttered something inaudible as she took the menu.

'What appeals to you most?' Marc repeated.
'Cheesecake, brandy snaps or strawberries and
cream?'

Jane choked.

'No, not the strawberries,' she said faintly. 'Anything but that.'

Marc gave her a strange look but luckily did not
question her.

They finished the rest of their meal in almost total
silence and on the drive home he seemed preoccupied. Jane was relieved to have a chance to
compose herself at last. After a while her turbulent
feelings began to subside and she decided that she was
probably just having a midlife crisis rather early.
Hormonal imbalance, that was it. But she must stop
it. Certainly Marc Le Rossignol was good-looking,
ruthless, with a negligent arrogance that would
probably inflame any red-blooded woman, but the
mere fact that she had a primitive physical response
to him did not mean that she was in love with him.
And only love could excuse the irrational way that
she was behaving. It was ridiculous, particularly since
she scarcely knew anything about him. He might even
be married or engaged already. This thought gave her
such a jolt that she blurted out the question before
she could stop herself.

'You're not married, are you?'

Marc looked taken aback.

'No. Why?'

Jane cringed.

'Oh. Uh. No reason. Just…you know…small talk,' she babbled.

You fool! she told herself savagely. You moron! What are you trying to do? Make him believe that you're the village idiot? While you're at it, why don't you tell him the truth and really shock him? Say something like, Oh, I just wondered if you're already taken because I'd like to go to bed with you myself. With a wild-eyed look she clamped her bottom teeth firmly over her upper lip for fear that the words would escape from her mouth. Marc glanced at her rather uneasily.

'Why are you pulling those strange faces?'

'I'm not,' she said hastily. 'I always look like this.'

'No, you don't. You're normally very pretty, but when you stick your jaw out like that you look like a wild animal trapped in a corner. Is it the terrifying word marriage that affects you that way?'

'No!' cried Jane.

'Perhaps you've been unhappily married yourself?' probed Marc.

'No! I've never been married and I don't intend to be.'

'Why not?' he demanded. 'Is it that you hate men? I can't help feeling that some bad experience must have soured your nature.'

'Do we have to keep talking about marriage?' asked Jane in an exasperated voice.

'Well, you started it,' pointed out Marc reasonably. 'You asked me if I was married.'

'Oh, forget it, will you? It was stupid of me to mention it. Anyway, my nature isn't soured!'

'Oh, I see,' murmured Marc. 'So these strange looks you give me do not represent hostility?'

'N-no,' stammered Jane.

'And you are actually perfectly friendly towards me?'

She turned away from him and stared out of the passenger window, feeling suddenly trapped. She couldn't come right out and say, I resent you bitterly for seizing my home and wrecking my dreams, but I feel a completely irrational sexual attraction to you. Instead she gave a sickly grin.

'Oh, yes, perfectly friendly,' she said in a failing voice.

Marc's hand shot out and gripped hers.

'Don't lie, Jane. I know you hate me. Let's be honest—there's a contest of wills going on here and quite a challenging one. You want to get rid of me and I intend to stay. But I warn you, I will be the winner.'

Jane fumed in silence for the rest of the trip home and could not wait to escape from Marc's hateful company. He did not drive all the way to the house immediately, but stopped the car just inside the entrance to the vineyard and climbed out to inspect the grapes. He tasted one and nodded thoughtfully.

'Come here,' he ordered.

Jane resented the curt summons but she too was interested in the condition of the grapes. She strolled across to join him and was just about to pick some fruit from the cluster when Marc popped a grape directly into her mouth. Even that brief touch of his fingers on her lips sent an unwelcome thrill through her so that she had to force herself to concentrate on the warm, sweet juice that was spilling on to her tongue.

'I think they'll be ready to harvest next week,' announced Marc. 'Do you agree?'

Jane nodded.

'And after that the real excitement begins,' he said with his eyes gleaming. 'We can start winemaking together.'

Jane tried hard not to be caught up in his anticipation.

'A lot might go wrong,' she said discouragingly. 'It could rain.'

'True, but if it turns out well I'll be very pleased. I'll probably stay here.'

Jane's mouth twisted.

'Well, I hope you don't expect me to wish you luck, then,' she said.

Marc gave an exasperated sigh and seized her arm. He seemed on the point of saying something, but then shook his head and gritted his teeth. When he did speak, his words were clipped and barely civil.

'Get in. I'll drive you the rest of the way,' he commanded.

Jane felt a little spurt of satisfaction at having annoyed him even that far. She pulled free of his grip.

'No, thanks. I'll walk from here.'

It wasn't far to the house, but the car was already parked outside and the back door was open when she arrived. Marc appeared to have vanished. Just as she came into the back porch she heard the ding of the fax machine in the study and quickened her pace. Marc came hurrying down the stairs and they collided in the hall.

'There's a fax,' said Jane.

'I know,' agreed Marc. 'I'm just going to get it.'

She opened her mouth to protest and then realised that it was entirely likely that the fax was for Marc and not for her. It was just one more unwelcome reminder that he was the legal occupant now and that she was living here on sufferance in her own home.

'You'd better come in here,' called Marc from the study. 'This concerns you too.'

'What?' asked Jane eagerly, hurrying in to join him. 'Is it from my father? Has something happened?'

'No, it's from Simone,' said Marc in an abstracted voice, looking down at the long sheet of paper in his hand.

'Who is Simone?' asked Jane with a sinking sensation.

Marc was still reading and a pleased expression had come over his face. There was a glimmer of amusement in his eyes when at last he looked up.

'Simone Cabanou. She's a neighbour of mine near Bordeaux,' he explained carelessly. 'She's coming to stay here at the farm to find out more about Australian vineyard practices.'

A renewed wave of bitterness rose in Jane's breast. Normally she loved having guests to stay but it infuriated her to feel that she was not even being consulted but merely informed about this particular guest. Obviously Marc didn't consider this place to be her home any more, but only his. Damn him!

'That's nice,' she said coldly. 'I'm so pleased.'

'Are you?' asked Marc, darting her a searching glance. 'I wonder.'

Simone arrived three days later. By then Jane had got over her misgivings enough to make all the preparations she would have made for any other guest.

Crisp sheets on the bed in the best spare room, gold and russet chrysanthemums in a crystal vase on the mantelpiece, a tin of chocolate wafers and a couple of juicy paperbacks on the bedside cupboard. Yet she still felt strangely reluctant to confront the mysterious Simone in person.

To her surprise, Marc tracked her down in mid-afternoon when she was checking the winemaking vats and asked her if she would like to go to the airport with him to meet their guest.

'All right,' she agreed, wiping her hands on her jeans. 'But wouldn't you rather be alone with her?'

Marc shrugged carelessly.

'I'll have plenty of time to be alone with her later,' he replied.

It was an answer which left Jane feeling vaguely dissatisfied. As they drove towards the airport she even managed to overcome her innate dislike of asking personal questions.

'Why is Simone really coming here?' she demanded bluntly.

Marc gazed out at the golden grass and blue hills that were gliding by and took his time about answering, as if he was more interested in the countryside than Simone.

'Partly curiosity, I think,' he said at last. 'We've known each other for a long time and she was very interested when I told her about this new venture of mine. We've been in touch quite a bit since I've been here. I think she may even try to persuade her family to introduce a few Australian innovations in their vineyard.'

'She comes from a winemaking family too?' asked Jane.

'Yes, they have a large vineyard near ours. Simone is a qualified accountant and she does all the financial side of the business. I was telling her only last week about the system of movable trellis wires that you use in Australia. It's standard practice here, but quite a revolutionary idea in France. She's very keen to find out how it's done and how much it can increase profits.'

'Oh,' said Jane, feeling slightly relieved. If Simone was only coming here for business reasons then perhaps she wouldn't stay too long. Although on the other hand the trip from Europe was so arduous that it was hardly worth making just for the sake of a few days.

'Will she be here very long?' she asked, trying to hide her eagerness for Simone's rapid departure.

Marc darted her a surprised look.

'She'll stay as long as she likes, of course,' he replied. 'We're ... old friends.'

Something in the way he said the word 'friends' made alarm bells ring in Jane's head. Friends? she thought suspiciously. Or something more? She was surprised at the pang of antagonism that went through her. She hadn't even met Simone and the poor woman might be very nice indeed. She tried to tell herself that her instinctive dislike was only due to resentment at the invasion of her home, but she had a niggling suspicion that what she was actually feeling was jealousy. How stupid! Marc didn't mean anything to her. He had merely kissed her once, which was an incident she was doing her best to forget. So why should it annoy her so much to learn that he and Simone were 'old friends'? It would be better to look on the bright side. With luck, Simone's report on the vineyard might prove so discouraging that they would both pack up and leave immediately. Yet somehow the thought of Marc's departure didn't make her feel quite as happy as she'd expected.

Simone's plane arrived on time, at four-fifteen p.m. on the dot. She was one of the first people to walk across the tarmac and Jane's heart sank when she saw her. The Frenchwoman looked as if she had stepped off a fashion-modelling catwalk rather than a horror flight from Europe. She was tall and slim, dressed in a cream trouser suit with scarlet grosgrain ribbon trim. Her dark hair was pulled back into a chignon, a style which showed off her swan-like neck and flawless features. Her make-up looked as if it had been done in a professional salon and she was festooned with various elegant accessories—gold and pearl earrings, an expensive gold watch, a Louis Vuitton handbag. Her brown eyes lit up at the sight of Marc and she smiled radiantly, revealing flawless white teeth.

'Marc!'

'Simone!'

As if moved by a common impulse they rushed into each other's arms, embraced fervently, and kissed each other on both cheeks. Jane, standing back a couple of paces, had to admit grudgingly that they made a stunningly handsome couple. Simone was almost as tall as Marc, and they both had the expensive, elusive aura of money and power and good taste. Once the initial embrace was over, a great torrent of French burst forth, far too rapid for Jane to follow. She stood woodenly, feeling like an insignificant dwarf dressed in the cast-off clothing from a charity shop. Even Simone's voice was enchanting—a melodious murmur that made several passing men turn around and stare admiringly. At last the quickfire volley of French came to a halt. Marc turned around, still smiling, gripped Jane's shoulder and pulled her forward.

'You must meet Jane,' he said in English. 'She's spent all morning preparing your room, Simone.'

'*Qui est-ce?*' asked Simone. '*C'est ta domestique?*'

'Speak English, *chérie*,' urged Marc reprovingly. 'Jane doesn't understand much French. No, she's not the housemaid. She's the daughter of the vineyard owner and she's still living on the property at the moment. It's a temporary arrangement, of course.'

'I see,' said Simone thoughtfully.

She extended one manicured hand with long, scarlet-tipped fingernails to Jane. There was little warmth in her handshake and her brown eyes were appraising rather than friendly. Not that Jane could really blame her for her lack of goodwill. Jane herself wasn't exactly brimming with sweetness at the moment either. Practically every word of Marc's speech had stung her in some way. She didn't like the thought that Simone had mistaken her for a housemaid and even less did she like the ominous statement that she was only staying on at the house as a temporary measure. Worse still was her growing suspicion about the nature of the relationship between Marc and Simone. Her French might be patchy but she knew enough to understand that '*chérie*' meant darling. Shaking Simone's hand as briefly as possible, she spoke in a voice that was cool and strained, quite unlike her usual tone.

'Welcome to Tasmania, Simone. I hope your stay here will be very happy.'

And brief, she added silently to herself.

CHAPTER FOUR

TENSION mounted over the next few days. In spite of Marc's explanation Simone did tend to treat Jane as the '*domestique*' around the house and Jane reacted by spending as much time as possible in the vineyard and the winery to escape from her. Not that this was an ideal solution, for she found herself tormented by doubts about what Simone and Marc were finding to talk about so earnestly in the house. It was not just movable trellises, she was sure of that.

A few days after Simone's arrival Jane walked into the sitting-room straight into the midst of another rapid-fire volley of French. Simone had the lapels of Marc's shirt in her hands and was staring at him with a distorted, impassioned expression on her lovely face while Marc looked back at her with a faint, weary frown. At the creak of the heavy cedar door they both stopped speaking and glanced sharply at Jane. Simone snatched away her hands from Marc's shirt, strode across the room with her breast heaving, paused to give Jane a venomous look and then walked out.

'Did I interrupt something?' asked Jane innocently.

'We were just discussing the costs per litre of stainless steel storage tanks,' replied Marc in a deadpan voice.

'It's amazing the things some people get upset about, isn't it?' demanded Jane.

'Amazing,' said Marc drily.

Jane let out an exasperated sigh. When it came to this sort of verbal fencing, Marc could beat her any day of the week. It was clear enough that he didn't want to discuss the issue any further, but some demon of curiosity goaded her on.

'Look, Marc,' she began, 'it's probably none of my business, but——'

'You're right. It is none of your business,' cut in Marc.

His bluntness infuriated her.

'There's no need to be so rude!' she flared. 'Simone is my guest in a way and if she's upset about something then I can't help being concerned about it. After all, it might have something to do with me.'

Marc took a sudden swift, harsh breath. His eyes were opaque and unfathomable as he looked down at her.

'It has everything to do with you,' he muttered. 'But it's still none of your business.'

His lips brushed hers briefly, then he went out of the room without a backward glance. Jane touched her mouth and shuddered. She could still feel the tingling warmth of his kiss, although it only left her mystified and unhappy. I want him, but I don't trust him, she thought miserably. I haven't the least idea of what's going on between him and Simone, but something definitely is. Oh, why did he ever come here?

Fortunately her thoughts were given a new direction the following morning by Marc's announcement that the grapes were ready to harvest. Immediately Jane went to the phone and began calling the people who had volunteered to work as pickers. There was no shortage of workers. Plenty of teenagers in the district were only too happy to earn some extra money and some of her old friends had offered to come along just for the fun of it.

The next morning they arrived shortly after dawn and Jane was kept busy for over an hour allocating buckets, secateurs and gardening gloves. After that the real work began—hours and hours of cutting the stems, dropping the bunches of grapes into buckets and emptying the buckets into large receiving bins. It was a pleasant job, with the sun beating down warmly and the green vine leaves rustling in a gently westerly breeze, but after lunch Jane's pace began to slow. By the end of the day her wrists were aching, her face and arms were sunburnt, her clothes were dusty and stained with juice. Worse still, hunger pains were attacking her so fiercely that several times she could have sworn she smelt the aroma of juicy spit-roasted beef.

'Do you think we ought to ask everyone to come into Richmond with us and have a counter meal?' she asked Marc wearily as they stood watching the last bin of grapes being hauled up to the winery by tractor. 'I'm starving.'

'I have a much better idea,' said Marc. 'I've decided to follow the old custom we have in Bordeaux. I've organised a dinner and dance for the grape-pickers.'

'A dinner and dance?' echoed Jane in alarm. 'But when ...? How ...? Who's doing the food and the music?'

'I've hired caterers and a bush dance band.'

'I can't possibly afford——' she began.

He laid two fingers warningly on her lips.

'It's my treat,' he said carelessly. 'Now, come on, we want everyone to assemble in the barn as soon as possible.'

As they came trudging up the last stretch of path towards the house Jane realised that the smell of barbecued beef hadn't been a hallucination after all. When Marc gave a party, he evidently did it in style. An entire steer was being barbecued on a spit just outside the barn, giving off an aroma that made her mouth water. From inside the barn came the sound of laughter and conversation and musical instruments tuning up.

'What are they all doing in there?' she asked. 'Am I the only one who didn't know about this party?'

Marc's eyes narrowed in amusement.

'As a matter of fact, you are,' he agreed tranquilly. 'I told everybody about it this morning while you were in the shed looking for extra secateurs and I swore them to secrecy. I wanted to surprise you.'

Jane felt unexpectedly stirred by this simple statement.

'You mean, you did this just to please me?' she asked with a catch in her voice.

'Oh, I wouldn't say that,' retorted Marc with a shrug. 'I just thought you might object if you knew, so I decided it was easier to do it without consulting you.'

Oh, great, thought Jane. He wasn't trying to please me at all, just being high-handed and arrogant and acting as if he owns the place. Before she could open her mouth to protest, Marc laid his hand on her shoulder and gave her a little push.

'Well, go on,' he ordered. 'You'd better get washed and changed so that you can enjoy yourself.'

Frowning thoughtfully, Jane made her way into the house. But she did no more than wash her face and hands and run a comb through her hair, which was full of dust and bits of vine leaves. It seemed unfair to put on good clothes when most of the pickers were still in the sweaty, grape-stained clothes they had worn for the harvest.

All the same, she felt at a distinct disadvantage ten minutes later when she arrived in the barn to see that Simone was wearing an expensive silk blouse teamed with a scarlet skirt that clung in dramatic folds around her long, slim legs. Not that Simone had become as hot and dirty as anybody else in any case. She had spent most of the day attired in a cream linen dress and straw hat, sitting under a grape arbour and writing down the weights of each new bin of grapes.

However, Marc, who was standing next to her, looked like a genuine worker. Like Jane, he had washed his face and hands and combed his hair, but his sleeves were rolled up, revealing muscular tanned forearms, and the front of his shirt was still stained with grape juice. Beneath the spicy tang of his after-shave lotion, he smelled of sun and earth and hot, crushed fruit. He greeted Jane with a careless smile, then strode away to a side table and returned with a tall crystal glass of champagne in either hand.

'You get one drink and after that I'm going to put you to work,' he warned. 'Here's to the success of our partnership and our vintage.'

Jane opened her mouth to argue and then thought better of it. This was hardly the moment to quibble about the use of words like 'our partnership', not with so many of her friends standing around eager for a really good party rather than ringside seats at a really good fight. She banished her misgivings, touched her glass against Marc's with a gentle chime and smiled uncertainly.

'To our partnership,' she said, and drank. The bubbles tingled on her tongue, then the excellence of the taste suddenly made itself felt and she gave a gasp of surprise. 'That's superb, Marc, what is it?'

'Veuve Clicquot,' he replied.

'Veuve Clicquot? The finest French champagne that exists? Have you really provided that for over forty people?'

'Why not? It's an occasion worth celebrating. Besides, the rest of the entertainment is pretty simple.'

Looking about her, Jane could see his point, but she also guessed shrewdly that the rustic scene before her had cost quite a lot of money to create. The barn was lit with paper lanterns, which cast a soft, peachy glow over the scene. In this dim light she saw that three long trestle tables had been arranged almost in the shape of a square with the fourth side left open. Two tables were spread with red and white checked cloths and sturdy but attractive maiolica crockery, along with expensive wine glasses of deceptive simplicity. The third table at the far end of the room was laden with an assortment of lavish salads, crusty French bread, potatoes baked in their jackets with sour cream and chives and an assortment of other dishes. A rostrum was set up against the fourth wall of the barn, containing the four members of a bush band. A few feet away from them an impromptu bar had been arranged in a corner.

'I'm just going to say a few words to welcome everyone,' murmured Marc, lowering his head so that he could speak into Jane's ear. 'After that I want it all to be casual and as much fun as possible, but I'd like you to help me by acting as bartender with me, if you're agreeable. I've got a good selection of wines for our guests to try and you can help answer any questions people might have about them.'

'All right,' agreed Jane, beginning to feel intrigued by the prospect. It looked as if this evening might be fun.

It was fun. Marc's speech of welcome was brief and witty, making everyone laugh. After that he and Jane set to work at the bar and were soon doing a brisk trade in pouring Tasmanian Chardonnay, Pinot Noir, Cabernet Sauvignon and Rhine Riesling, while explaining the finest points of each. The food was excellent and, after dessert and coffee were brought in, the bush band struck up some lively reels and jigs. Jane went back for a second helping of lemon meringue pie, but was soon called to the bar by Marc to help him dispense Australian port, Tokay and muscat to go with the coffee. When everybody else had been served she helped herself to a glass of muscat so thick and concentrated that it painted the sides of the glass.

'Mmm, I love that stuff,' she said appreciatively as she swallowed the last drop of sweet, sticky liquid.

'Well, I don't think we can manage to make muscat here,' said Marc. 'But it's formidable to think that next year we may be drinking our own Chardonnay, isn't it?'

Next year we may be drinking our own Chardonnay. The words reverberated in Jane's head. It sounded as if Marc had already made his decision about whether to purchase the property. Yet, looking into his glowing brown eyes, Jane did not feel the pang of dismay that she expected, but only a heady rush of excitement at the prospect that he would still be here beside her in a year's time.

'Do you really think you're going to buy the place and stay here?' she asked.

'Why not?' he replied. 'It has some interesting possibilities.'

At that moment Jane became aware that someone was standing at the bar waiting to be served. She swung round and saw that it was Simone, with her empty port glass held out and a smile on her face that did not quite reach her eyes.

'I couldn't help overhearing you, Marc,' she said sweetly. 'But even if you do buy the property, there's really no need for you to be here yourself. You could put a manager in to run the place. Your own time is far too valuable to waste in a backwater like this.'

Marc refilled her glass and handed it back to her.

'I don't know, Simone,' he said thoughtfully. 'I'm rather taken by Tasmania. I think I might enjoy living here for half the year.'

Simone said something sharp in French and once again the conversation stampeded away at a pace that Jane couldn't follow. But Simone's flashing dark eyes, tight-lipped smile and rapid, shallow breathing showed clearly that she was becoming upset. At last, with an obvious effort, the Frenchwoman took a deep breath, smiled sweetly and set down her untouched glass of port.

'I wonder if you could spare Jane for a moment,' she said in English to Marc. 'It looks as though I'll have to fly back to France quite soon, and there are one or two financial details about the property that I'd like to discuss with her.'

'Wouldn't tomorrow morning be better?' countered Marc.

'Now,' insisted Simone.

Jane felt a surge of glee at the news that Simone would soon be leaving, but her joy was soon quenched when she followed the other woman out into the garden. Although it had been a warm day, there was now a distinct chill in the evening air and by common accord they made their way down to the glowing fire which had been used to barbecue the steer. In the glow from the leaping orange flames Jane saw that Simone's face still looked angry and turbulent, although she was obviously struggling to preserve an air of calm.

'What do you want to talk to me about?' she asked curiously.

Simone waved to a wooden picnic table and garden benches set under one of the trees. In the distance they could hear the muted uproar of the party in the barn but overhead the night sky was dark and spangled with stars while the sweet perfume of early narcissus hung in the air. Simone seemed to pause and gather her thoughts before she answered.

'I want to do you a favour,' she said at last, in an ingratiating voice.

'What kind of a favour?' asked Jane suspiciously.

'I'm an accountant. Marc trusts my financial advice and he has told me all about the way you handed over control of your funds to your father and sank your assets into a property that doesn't legally belong to you. It was pure madness, of course, but I think I can persuade Marc not to go ahead with the purchase of the vineyard. Naturally you'll still have to get a good lawyer to regain control of your money, but——'

Jane was no longer listening. She felt a sick, breathless sensation, as if someone had just punched her in the stomach. In spite of her initial antagonism towards Marc, she realised that she had begun to like and trust him. Now she felt a sense of horrifying betrayal to learn that he had discussed her private affairs with an outsider. Even if Simone was an accountant and his close friend, did he have to humiliate Jane by revealing how naïve and gullible she had been? And what business was it of Simone's anyway?

'Why don't you want him to buy Saddler's Corner?' she cut in.

Simone seemed taken aback by the sharp edge in her voice.

'I thought you'd be pleased at the idea,' she protested. 'It's what you want, isn't it?'

Jane was silent for a moment, thinking about that. Was it what she wanted? Three weeks ago she would have jumped for joy at the thought of getting Marc off her land and never seeing him again. Now she wasn't quite so sure...

'Maybe,' she replied curtly.

'You don't sound very pleased,' complained Simone. 'I thought you'd be delighted at the idea. Marc was so eloquent about how much you loved this place and how hard you'd worked on it that he brought tears to my eyes.'

I'll bet, thought Jane fiercely. The only time she could ever imagine Simone having tears in her eyes was if she had lost a million francs on a financial transaction or broken a heel on one of her crocodile skin shoes.

'What's in it for you if Marc doesn't buy the place?' she asked.

'Nothing,' replied Simone, her eyes widening. 'I just want to do you a favour and prevent Marc from taking a big financial risk. It would give me great pleasure if I could be of help to both of you.'

'Well, I appreciate your generosity,' said Jane with a touch of sarcasm as she rose to her feet. 'But I don't think there's any need for you to use your influence. I'd rather sort the matter out with Marc myself.'

She turned to go, but Simone caught her arm.

'Wait! I suppose it's true that I do have a personal stake in this matter. I didn't want to discuss my private affairs, but you leave me no choice. All right, I'll be perfectly honest with you, Jane. Marc and I intend to marry and I don't like the way you're pursuing him.'

Jane was so angry that she could have slapped Simone's face.

'I'm not pursuing him!' she blazed. 'If anything, he's——'

She broke off, unwilling to reveal her own secret. That kiss was something between her and Marc, nobody else.

'If anything he's pursuing you?' finished Simone with a touch of malice. 'That doesn't surprise me.'

'Doesn't it?' asked Jane in horror. 'But if you're planning to marry him, surely you don't expect him to go around chasing other women?'

Simone laughed, a brittle sound like the breaking of crystal.

'What a sweet, idealistic nature you have,' she said. 'He's a man, after all. Any sensible woman turns a blind eye to these little affairs.'

'I wouldn't!' cried Jane hotly.

Simone shrugged, as if her point had just been proved.

'No, you obviously take life very seriously, which is exactly why I don't want you to get hurt by having an affair with Marc, my dear.'

'Really?' asked Jane sceptically. 'You lie awake at night, do you, thinking to yourself, "Well, how can I save poor little Jane West from getting hurt by plunging into a meaningless affair with Marc Le Rossignol?" That's kind of you!'

'You're not quite so naïve as you look, are you?'

'No,' said Jane stonily.

Simone nodded thoughtfully, as if they had reached a new stage in their negotiations. Then she gestured to the picnic table.

'Do sit down again and let's discuss this matter calmly. Would you like a cigarette?'

'I don't smoke.'

Jane looked at Simone's opal-studded lighter with dislike. Why did everything the other woman owned have to proclaim her wealth and status and good taste? Power-dressing to impress the ignorant peasants, no doubt! I suppose she clips her toenails with a pair of gold-handled scissors, she thought sourly.

'All right,' said Simone, blowing out a cloud of smoke. 'Let's be open with each other. If you have an affair with Marc, you will get hurt. Frankly I don't care if you do. What I do care about is the thought of Marc wasting time and money here at the end of the world when he should be in Europe with me.'

'And what makes you think I'm going to have an affair with Marc?'

'Mainly that look of doggy devotion in your eyes when he comes into the room,' said Simone in an amused voice. 'Oh, I don't blame you. He's a very attractive man. Scores of starry-eyed young women have fallen for him in the past and he enjoys their admiration. The sad thing is that it's just a game to him. He's quite happy to offer them a few weeks of breathless passion, but he always comes back to me in the end.'

'I don't believe you!' cried Jane hotly. 'I'm sure Marc's not like that. And anyway, you can't possibly love him or you wouldn't talk about him so scathingly.'

Simone snorted.

'Love!' she echoed. 'There's a lot more to life than love, as you'll find out one of these days. My relationship with Marc is not just a matter of love; there are all sorts of things that bind us together. We speak the same language, we come from the same environment, we understand each other. A marriage between us will work, whereas Marc would never dream of having anything more than a brief, meaningless liaison with you.'

'Well, how do I know that he genuinely plans to marry you?' asked Jane, her voice rising and growing more rapid. 'I only have your word for it. I can easily ask him whether it's true or not.'

For a moment Simone looked taken aback, then she shrugged indifferently.

'Do so, if you wish,' she invited. 'Although he'll probably deny it anyway. He's not a man who likes to be hemmed in by possessive women and you'll only make yourself look ridiculous by pestering him with questions. You'd be much wiser to preserve your own dignity and drop him. I promise that I'll persuade him to relinquish your vineyard if you do.'

'No,' said Jane flatly, jumping to her feet again. 'I'm not making any deals with you, Simone. Marc's not some kind of prize for us to haggle over. He's a grown man who can make his own choices in business or love without any help from you. Besides, I don't believe any of the hateful things you've said about him and I think you've got a cheek trying to interfere in my private life. Now please excuse me, I have guests to consider.'

In spite of her defiant words, Jane felt as if a poisoned thorn had worked its way under her skin as she made her way back to the house. The moment she entered the barn her gaze scanned the crowd in search of Marc. When she did manage to locate him a prickle of uneasiness went through her. He was standing in the corner by the bar, talking to an attractive red-headed girl who looked about twenty-one years old. Marc had one arm around her shoulders and their heads were close together. There was a suggestion of intimacy about the two figures which filled Jane with apprehension. Was she witnessing exactly the sort of scene that Simone had tried to warn her about? Or had Simone's comments been mere spite designed to make her see harm in a perfectly innocent conversation? She simply didn't know and the sense of doubt tormented her.

She tried to work her way around the tables unobtrusively so that she could get a closer look at Marc and the girl. Was it her imagination or did he have a sultry expression in his eyes as he came back with fresh glasses of wine for both of them? Jane was just trying to edge closer to see when someone grabbed her arm, making her jump. She swung round.

'Oh, Brett!' she exclaimed. 'You startled me.'

It was a relief to see Brett's sunburnt beaming face. At least he was open and honest and uncomplicated. If she had any sense, she'd marry him instead of yearning for a ruthless heartbreaker like Marc. Perhaps she ought to invite Brett over for a meal some time or ask him if he'd like to go to a film with her. Or would it be unkind to encourage him when her own feelings were in such turmoil?

'Brett——' she began.

She got no further. Reaching out with one massive red hand, Brett dragged a tall, buxom, black-haired girl towards him and grinned at both of them.

'I've been looking for you everywhere, Jane,' he said cheerfully. 'I want to introduce Karen to you. I met her up in Surfers Paradise while I was away on holiday a few weeks ago. She said she might be coming down to Tassie herself, so I gave her my address. I never thought she'd take me up on it, but here she is! She's staying at the farm for a few days with me, but she likes the place so much she reckons she might stick around and look for a job. She's a nurse, so she can probably get employment anywhere. Karen, this is my old mate, Jane. We used to climb trees together and that sort of thing when we were kids.'

Jane felt a brief, ridiculous twinge of self-pity as she shook hands with Karen. The other girl had a wide, engaging smile and from the fond way she was looking at Brett it wasn't hard to guess that a promising romance was budding between them. Jane was pleased for both of them, but she couldn't help feeling a bit forlorn as well. It looked as though her one faithful admirer had finally deserted her.

'Hello, Karen,' she said. 'It's lovely to meet you.'

For the rest of the evening Jane did her best to join
in the party atmosphere. She bounced around to the
music of banjos and tin whistles; she went around
from group to group, making sure that she had a chat
with everyone; she pressed food and soft drinks on
people and she made up impromptu beds in the house
for three or four children who had come along with
their parents for the harvest and were now drooping
with exhaustion. Yet all the time that she was moving
around, acting the part of hostess, her eyes kept
straying to Marc and there was a curious, tight, aching
feeling in her chest.

It was not until the last guest had departed and the
caterers had cleaned up and gone away that she
realised just what she was feeling. Although she had
a flight to catch the following day, Simone had stayed
up late and was staying close to Marc, with the alert,
watchful look of a fierce guard-dog. Seeing them
together, Jane felt a wave of desolation sweep over
her. I know what's wrong with me, she thought bitterly. I'm in love with him. What a fool I am! I'm in
love with him . . .

When Jane awoke late the following morning, Marc
and Simone had already left for the airport. It was a
relief to be able to wander around the house, alone
with her own turbulent thoughts and feelings. All the
same, she could not help feeling anxious about what
would happen on Marc's return. Would she be able
to hide the embarrassing secret of her true feelings
for him? Or would he take one look at her face and
know everything?

As it happened, the ordeal proved much easier than
she had feared. When Marc returned he had nothing

on his mind other than work. There was no thought of kisses or highly-charged emotional scenes, no room for anything except long, painstaking hours of work in the winery.

'Ready to start winemaking?' he asked, the moment he was inside the door.

'Yes!' agreed Jane fervently. 'I can't wait.'

'I drive myself hard when I'm working,' he warned. 'And I expect to do the same to you. Can you take the pace?'

'Just watch me!' challenged Jane.

Marc was as good as his word. For the next twenty-eight days they both breathed, ate, slept and dreamed winemaking. First the grapes had to be crushed, then the red wines fermented 'on their skins' while the white grapes were placed in the press before fermentation. Sulphur dioxide, ascorbic acid and tartaric acid had to be added and they were kept constantly busy.

At last, after a month of ceaseless work, all the wine was safely in barrels and ready to be left for the next year to mature. To celebrate the successful conclusion of the first stage of their enterprise, Marc took Jane out to dinner at a local restaurant and ordered a bottle of the finest French champagne.

'I think we deserve a holiday after this,' he said. 'Well, a working holiday. What do you say to the idea of leaving Charlie Kendall in charge here and going on a tour of the other Tasmanian vineyards together?'

CHAPTER FIVE

JANE'S eyes dilated in surprise as she gradually took in the implications of what Marc was suggesting. Being in each other's company night and day, cooped up in a car or staying in motels, thrust into a highly-charged intimacy even worse than what they had experienced here.

'But . . . that would take several days,' she pointed out.

Marc seemed to enjoy her discomfiture. An unholy amusement gleamed in his brown eyes as she let his gaze travel slowly down over the low-cut neck of her best evening frock.

'So it would,' he marvelled. 'Why didn't I think of that? Could it be because this is the late twentieth century or because we're both grown-ups and have already been sharing a house for the last seven weeks with no ill-effects?'

Jane flushed to the roots of her hair at his mocking tone. With no ill-effects! she thought bleakly. Speak for yourself, Marc Le Rossignol. I've never been more tormented in my life than I have over the last seven weeks! She ignored the small voice deep inside her that told her she had never been more breathtakingly happy, either . . .

'Stop making fun of me!' she cried in exasperation. 'It's not easy travelling with other people, especially if you don't know them well. You can get under each other's skin over the slightest things.'

'Ah, yes,' agreed Marc, sipping his champagne reflectively. 'You, for instance, get under my skin a good deal of the time.'

Jane's heart lurched and then began to beat violently as she saw his narrowed eyes appraising her in the soft glow of the lamplight. Did he mean...? Could he possibly mean...? His whole body seemed to emanate a burning current of attraction that drew her insistently towards him. She leaned forward, her lips parted, her breath coming in a shallow, uneven rhythm, aware only that he was looking at her with a primitive, naked hunger in his eyes. He wants me! she thought exultantly. He wants me just as badly as I want him! And she did want him; there was no doubt of that. A deep, hot tide of wanting was throbbing through every inch of her body. The very air around them seemed to blaze and crackle with their mutual need. Then suddenly Marc dropped his eyelids and, when he looked up again, his entire expression had changed. His face wore its usual air of weary amusement.

'There are so many things you do that get under my skin,' he continued blandly. 'You leave wet towels on the bathroom floor, you never wash up after you use the kitchen, you play atrocious pop music late at night. But still there is a certain something about you... Yes, there is a certain something. I think I could bear your company for a week or so while we go around the wineries. If you're worried about protecting your modesty then naturally there will be separate bedrooms.'

Jane began to seethe quietly.

'I wish you'd stop going on about my modesty!' she flared. 'You make me sound like some virgin heroine in a Victorian melodrama and, let me tell you, that's a long way from the truth! Naturally I'll insist on separate bedrooms if we go, but not because I'm going to blush and swoon if you catch a glimpse of my ankle. It just so happens, while we're on the subject of my wet towels and things, that you have some rather awful habits too! Like the way you keep tidying up the study so I can never find anything any more. And the way you have to set the table with everything in perfect order and the knives and forks absolutely symmetrical before you can even sit down to eat. It drives me mad!'

Too late, she saw the twitch of amusement at the corners of his mouth and realised that he was deliberately baiting her.

'You wretch! You do it deliberately, don't you?' she protested. 'You set traps for me and wait for me to fall in!'

Marc acknowledged the truth of this with a sly wink that made Jane catch her breath. Why did he have to look so heartbreakingly gorgeous? With those long creases that formed in his cheeks when he smiled and the tough mouth with its ironic twist, he was practically irresistible! No woman could live in the house of a man so blatantly virile and sensual without feeling a heightened sense of her own power and femininity and mystery! She was beginning to think that the only way to save her sanity was to put a vast physical distance between them. No doubt it would be much wiser if she didn't go along on this trip, although she couldn't help feeling a sense of mingled pleasure and apprehension at the thought of exploring the island with him.

No. No! She must be hard-headed about it and stay out of his reach. Her life was difficult enough at the moment, with the uncertainty of the vineyard's future hanging over her, and she certainly didn't need the kind of dangerous complications that a week's touring with Marc might produce. A stormy expression came into her green eyes and she reached for the bottle in the ice-bucket and poured herself a second glass of champagne.

'Why don't you go on your own?' she asked bluntly.

Marc's eyebrows rose.

'That's not very friendly,' he chided her. 'I thought you could show me around. After all, I'll be leaving pretty soon and we may not see much more of each other.'

Jane's spirits took a sickening plunge, as though a trapdoor had just opened abruptly under her feet.

'Y-you're leaving?' she stammered. 'But why are you going so soon? There's another month or more until your option to purchase ends.'

Marc too reached for the champagne, poured some into his glass and sipped reflectively before he answered.

'Simone and I stayed up late talking the night before she left,' he said. 'She convinced me that there were urgent financial matters I needed to attend to in France. I promised her I'd return and sort everything out there once the winemaking was over.'

'Oh,' said Jane in a stricken voice.

She lowered her eyes to hide her despair. So Simone had won! Obviously she had been determined to remove Marc from Jane's influence, and the ease with which he had given way showed how strong the Frenchwoman's hold was over him. Her shock and

disappointment were so great that for a moment she
made no attempt to hide them.

'Will you be coming back?' she blurted out.

'Maybe.'

'Well, what's the point of going on a tour of the
Tasmanian wineries if you're only going to put a
manager in the vineyard here? Or not even buy it at
all?' she blazed. 'I thought you said you liked this
place.'

'I do,' agreed Marc mildly. 'I think it's a charming
island, full of charming people. And the most
charming inhabitant of all is a little spitfire of a
strawberry blonde with amazing green eyes and a terrible temper. Of course she has her virtues too. She
works eighteen hours a day without complaining, and
I think she deserves a little holiday now that the worst
of the work is over. So won't you come with me,
chérie?'

As he said this he reached forward and wound one
of Jane's curls around his finger. She jerked herself
free and tossed her head angrily, so that her hair
rippled and crackled around her shoulders. Did he
think she'd come down in the last rainshower? Obviously all that he had in mind was a little sexual frolic
before he returned to France to the woman he really
intended to marry. Well, knowing this made it easier
to make up her mind. There was no way Jane was
going to be fool enough to go to bed with Marc when
he was planning to leave the country in a few days'
time. She paused, struck by a sudden thought. If Marc
genuinely was leaving so soon, then there was really
no reason why she should deny herself the chance to
go on this tour of the vineyards in his company. It
wasn't as if anything dramatic would happen between

them. Besides, it would give her the chance to show him that she wasn't panting with eagerness to jump into his bed, that she saw him only as a fellow wine-maker. A dangerous smile curved her lips.

'That's very kind of you,' she said demurely.

Marc frowned.

'I never trust you when you're being meek,' he complained. 'But tell me, what's your answer? Are you coming?'

Jane picked up her champagne glass and tossed off the wine in a a single gulp so that a heady surge of bubbles seemed to race like wildfire through her veins. Then she gave Marc a long, slow, challenging stare.

'Yes,' she said.

Five days later, Jane sat watching Marc thoughtfully as he sent the Saab gliding effortlessly round the curves of the highway that led down the east coast of Tasmania. He was a good driver, but that didn't sur-prise her. He seemed to be good at so many things. It had filled her with a growing sense of despair over the last five days to realise just how effortlessly Marc Le Rossignol excelled in everything he did. In the course of their trip around the island Jane had dis-covered that he was a superb dancer, a skilful horseman and powerful swimmer, as well as a con-noisseur of wine and a brilliant linguist.

They had gone trail-riding through the scented, sunlit forests of the Huon Valley, eaten breakfast in the revolving restaurant at the Wrest Point casino while they watched the sun rise dramatically over the Hobart harbour, and spent a memorable afternoon tasting wines at the Pipers Brook vineyard with a group of Japanese tourists before going on to a dinner dance at the Launceston Country Club. Yet the memory which remained most vividly with Jane was the image of Marc carrying a little girl with a cut foot two hundred metres along the beach at Coles Bay to her mother.

The adoring look on the tearful child's face as she had clung to him had made Jane wonder if she had seriously misjudged him. Even if he was a ruthless flirt and a hard-headed businessman, she was beginning to suspect that underneath he was something more than that. A man who liked children, who really cared about them, who could be relied upon to be protective and tender when the circumstances demanded it. Stop it! Jane told herself. You're making him out to be some kind of saint and he isn't that. It's dangerous to start idealising him.

Deliberately she tore her gaze away from Marc, and looked out of the window at the jade-green sea and the dazzling white beaches flashing past them. It was warm in the car, too warm. She wound down the window and was immediately assaulted by the roar of pounding surf and the clean, aromatic scent of eucalyptus trees. Marc glanced across at her and smiled.

'This place is amazing,' he said. 'Miles and miles of white sandy beaches and hardly a person in sight.'

'It's nearly winter time,' Jane pointed out.

'But not very cold,' Marc replied. 'Even if the water's too chilly for swimming, the weather's very mild and sunny. You'd think people would be out in droves, but instead the place is practically deserted. It makes me feel as if we were the only man and woman on earth.'

I wish we were, thought Jane, with an odd, fluttering sensation in the pit of her stomach. Then I wouldn't have to worry about somebody else taking you away from me. You'd be all mine. It perturbed her to realise that, in spite of all her good intentions, she was more attracted to Marc than ever. I'll miss him so much when he goes, she thought. I don't know how I can bear it. Yet outwardly she gave no sign of her feelings.

'Don't count on the good weather holding,' she warned. 'Five days in a row must already be close to a record.'

Marc gave a low growl of laughter.

'Well, let's just hope it lasts long enough for us to see Maria Island,' he said. 'Didn't you say an Italian tried to establish a vineyard there nearly a century ago?'

'That's right,' agreed Jane. 'Although there are only ruins there now. Diego Bernacchi settled there at the beginning of this century and tried to grow vines. Unfortunately most Australians weren't interested in drinking wine then, but luckily things have changed today.'

'Obviously a man before his time,' commented Marc. 'Well, I hope you and I can make it together where he failed.'

I hope you and I can make it together—the words stung Jane with their poignancy. It was the sort of thing Marc might have said to her if they had been contemplating a future life together, or even marriage. But if he married anyone it would be Simone Cabanou, not Jane West. Still, she couldn't just sit here looking stricken and preoccupied. With an effort she found her voice.

'I hope so too,' she said.

'I think we'll get settled in Orford first,' continued
Marc. 'Then drive back to Triabunna and catch the
ferry to the island.'

'Where are we staying tonight?' asked Jane listlessly.

'I've booked into a colonial cottage. I know the big
hotels are fun, but I prefer something more homely,
don't you?'

'I suppose so,' muttered Jane in a troubled voice.
The last thing she wanted at the moment was a cosy
little place with log fires and chintz armchairs and
absolutely no other people to provide a diversion. At
least there was safety in numbers. In a big hotel, surrounded by hordes of other people, she did not have
to fear that she would lose her head and reveal her
true feelings!

He frowned at the lack of enthusiasm in her tone,
but said nothing.

When they reached the cottage just outside Orford
Jane saw that it had exactly the kind of ambience that
she feared. There was a garden where winter jasmine
hung in fragrant willows on a white picket fence; the
veranda had a trim of iron lace and there was a pol-
ished copper nameplate in the mellow sandstone next
to the front door, while the interior featured brass
beds, patchwork quilts, fresh flowers on the dining-
table, handmade chocolates in a basket in the kitchen
and a collection of Gershwin musicals by the cassette
deck. If they had been genuine lovers Jane would have
been in raptures at the place. As it was, she found the
atmosphere extremely threatening. Of course, Marc
would like it! It was just the sort of intimate little
love-nest where he could turn up the heat and try to
seduce her before he went away forever. In fact, he
had probably chosen the place for that very purpose.

But Jane saw it only as a scented trap which made her skin prickle with alarm.

'What's wrong? Don't you like it?' asked Marc, seeing her suspicious expression as she prowled from room to room.

'It's OK,' she said indifferently. 'Personally I prefer a water-bed, rock music and some junk sculpture.'

Marc winced.

'Do you really like that sort of stuff?' he asked incredulously.

'Sure. Why not?' lied Jane, whose true tastes ran to white lace pillowcases, intimate firelit dinners and dancing the tango.

'I don't understand heavy metal music,' groaned Marc. 'Or modern art, for that matter.'

'Well, you wouldn't, would you?' asked Jane sweetly. 'You've got to remember the generation gap.'

'Generation gap!' he echoed. 'Seven years' age difference is hardly a generation gap! And, if it is, there are ways of closing it.'

As he said this his voice dropped a semitone and a smoky, sensual look came into his eyes. Reaching out one hard brown hand, he traced a whorl on Jane's cheek with his thumb. A quiver went through her and she closed her eyes for an instant, but then remembered her resolve to keep him at arm's length.

'We'll miss the ferry,' she reminded him.

Before long they were out on the water, with the wake of the ferry vanishing behind them. Seagulls glided overhead, there was a smell of salt air, and the throb of the boat's engines made it vibrate like a live thing as it skimmed across the dazzling blue water of the channel. A profound hush seemed to settle on them when they came ashore.

'It's like stepping back in time,' marvelled Marc, looking around him. 'No roads, no shops. There's not even a permanent population, is there?'

'Only the ranger and his family,' replied Jane.

They both loved the pristine beauty of the island, drowsy and peaceful in the sun, although there were reminders of the more troubled past. The ruins of the convict settlement at Darlington stood eerie and deserted with its rows of cells and empty administrative quarters. And once, from the top of a rise, they glimpsed an abandoned farmhouse being slowly engulfed by a creeping tide of vegetation. But, for the two winemakers, the most fascinating remains of all were the traces of Diego Bernacchi's vineyard.

'I hope ours will do better than this,' said Marc, shading his eyes and looking down across the dense bracken to the blue sea beyond. 'I'd like to think that in five hundred years our winery would still be operating, just like my family's place in France.'

Jane felt a bittersweet tinge of emotion as she stood beside him. If they had been genuine lovers, she would have put her arm around his waist and laid her head on his shoulder and assured him fervently of her faith in their future. Instead she stood stiffly apart from him and yearned with all her heart to be in his arms.

The weather was growing distinctly colder on the trip back to Triabunna. The waves were steely-grey with white crests and there was a strong headwind blowing off the land so that they hit each wave with a choppy impact. Once ashore, they were grateful to get inside the warmth of the car and drive back to their cottage. Marc lit the fire which was already laid in the glass-sided wood heater and drew the curtains. As the kindling began to crackle and orange tongues of flame leaped up the flue he turned to Jane with a questioning look.

'What do you think? Shall we stay home tonight and cook something ourselves for dinner?'

'Oh, the weather's not really too bad,' protested Jane, who found the invitation distinctly alarming. 'I'd rather go out somewhere.'

'All right,' agreed Marc. 'We'll have dinner at the restaurant on the headland. But I'm warning you, if it does rain, then you will make breakfast tomorrow. And wash up.'

Marc looked triumphantly at her an hour later. They had just finished their smoked salmon entrées and were gazing out of the uncurtained restaurant windows when there was a sudden noise like the thunder of distant hooves and the dark, tossing seas beneath them vanished in a blur of driving rain.

'I'll have fruit yoghurt, cereal, eggs and bacon, orange juice and percolated coffee,' he announced in a smug voice.

The waitress, who had just come to take away their empty plates, looked startled.

'Are you sure, sir?' she asked. 'I've already ordered the beef tournedos with vegetables for you, but I suppose we can change it.'

Jane dissolved into helpless giggles and almost choked as a harassed-looking Marc attempted to explain. She was still giggling weakly when the bemused waitress finally beat a retreat. Marc scowled at her.

'I suppose you enjoy seeing me make a fool of myself?'

'I do,' she agreed blithely. 'It's a change from always seeing you being perfect.'

Marc's face shadowed and his eyes grew sombre.

'I'm far from perfect,' he growled. 'If I were perfect, I wouldn't be having the thoughts I'm having right now.'

'What thoughts?' asked Jane unwisely.

He leaned forward and spoke in a hoarse, sibilant murmur, so low that only she could hear it.

'I'm thinking that I'd like to take you back to the cottage, undress you slowly in the firelight and kiss every inch of your body until you were burning with desire for me, just as I am for you. And then I'd drive deep, deep inside you, until you started to thresh and moan and cling to me. And finally your whole body would convulse and you'd cry out my name, and I'd know that you were truly mine.'

Jane's breath caught in her throat, her eyes dilated and her heart began to beat in a suffocating rhythm.

'Marc, don't!' she begged huskily. 'Don't joke like that.'

'I'm not joking,' he said through his teeth. 'It's what I want, Jane, and you know it. It's what you want too.'

'It isn't,' she whispered. 'It isn't.'

But it was. Even as he spoke, his words seemed to have tripped some switch inside her, so that her whole body was pulsating with a tingling current of desire. Her breath came in shallow flutters and her pulses were racing, while a dark heat seemed to uncurl and throb deep within her. Although she was urging him to stop saying these delicious forbidden things, she found that she was leaning towards him with her lips parted and her breasts thrust forward. Shock and dismay made her stiffen and then shrink back in her seat, with her eyes lowered and her cheeks flushed.

Marc reached out and took her hand, running his fingers caressingly down the back of it.

'You see?' he murmured. 'Lie to me if you like, but your own body betrays you.'

Fortunately, at that moment, the waitress arrived with Marc's Tournedos chasseur and Jane's steak *au poivre*. During the ensuing ritual of sampling the burgundy which Marc had chosen to accompany the meal and then sinking her teeth into the juicy, peppery beef, Jane was able to forget the passion which had blazed up between them. Even her fear that Marc would raise the subject again after the waitress left proved unfounded. Instead they talked about overseas holidays, Australian cuisine, grape varieties and their favourite films. By the time they left the restaurant Jane felt safe and relaxed, which was a serious mistake.

The rain was still falling in a steady, soaking downpour when they reached the cottage and the fragrance of wet earth and drenched flowers filled Jane's nostrils as she stood huddled and shivering on the veranda. Marc inserted the key in the lock and held the front door open for Jane to enter the house. She turned on the hall light and Marc followed her inside and stood patiently waiting as she took off her damp coat. She had just enough time to glimpse the mahogany sideboard, with the vase of jonquils standing on it and the gold-framed mirror hanging on the wall above it, before the light flickered and went out. Jane, who had one arm trapped in her sleeve, gave a cry of surprise and Marc gripped her shoulder reassuringly. She stiffened and caught her breath at his touch. It was the kind of reassurance that she found more alarming than helpful. In the unexpected darkness she was intensely conscious of the warmth and size and masculinity of his body so close to hers.

'Don't worry,' he said calmly. 'It's probably just a fuse, unless the storm has brought some wires down somewhere. I'll soon fix it.'

'How will you see?' she asked.

'There are some candles and matches in the third drawer next to the fridge in the kitchen,' he replied.

Jane gave a muffled giggle. Trust Marc to notice something like that! Feeling like Houdini, she finally escaped from her coat, then felt her way gingerly to the row of brass hooks on the wall and hung it up. A moment later the damp softness of Marc's cashmere overcoat brushed against her as he did the same.

'Ready for the big adventure?' he asked.

Without waiting for a reply, he took her left hand and together they groped their way down the hall. She found the warmth of Marc's grip unsettling. Instead, she tried to concentrate on the other sensations that she was noticing. The drumming of rain on the tin roof, the roar and shriek of the wind, the softness of carpet underfoot, the carved newels of the staircase that suddenly met her questing fingers, the scent of rose pot pourri that wafted out from the dining-room doorway. There was something primitive about total darkness, something about its dense, black, enfolding quality that made her want to cling to Marc as if hidden terrors might be lurking out of sight. Ancient childhood nightmares of witches and monsters and huge, hairy, poisonous spiders began to teem in her head. When her hand brushed against something damp and cold and clinging at the foot of the stairs she gave a startled shriek.

'What's wrong?' asked Marc.

'Something grabbed me.'

She felt his muscles bunch and harden as he reached to investigate. Then a groan of laughter escaped him.

'It's that wet towel you left hanging over the banisters,' he said in an exasperated voice.

'Oops,' mumbled Jane.

After that they reached the kitchen safely without being bitten or devoured or changed into creepy crawlies by any magic wands. Marc released her hand and located the candles and matches. There was a scraping sound, then the room was filled with a friendly, flickering gold light and the world suddenly seemed safe and welcoming again. Marc looked at her with an incredulous lift of his eyebrows.

'How could you possibly believe something had grabbed you?' he asked. 'There's nobody here but us.'

'If you laugh at me, I'll hit you!' warned Jane, her eyes flashing. 'It just so happens that occasionally I have an irrational fear of the dark, especially when I'm taken unawares.'

'Don't worry, *chérie*. I'll protect you,' promised Marc with just a hint of mockery. 'Why don't you go into the living-room? There should still be some light from the fire there, unless it's gone out. I'll see if I can mend the fuse and then come and join you.'

Taking a candle, Jane padded out of the kitchen into the living-room, which had been added on at the back of the house. A comforting red glow still came from the glass firebox and she sat on the couch with a sigh of relief. It was so cosy here that she almost felt like going to sleep. Kicking off her shoes, she curled up with her legs beside her and gazed into the fire. She was already drifting in a warm, dreamlike trance when Marc rejoined her a few minutes later.

'How did you go with the fuse?' she asked. 'Is it fixed?'

He shook his head.

'No luck, I'm afraid. There must be a wire down somewhere. Would you like a glass of port before we go to bed?'

'Mmm, please.'

Marc put two more logs on the fire and poured the drinks.

'Move your legs,' he ordered companionably, and sat beside her.

I wish it could be like this always, thought Jane with a bittersweet twinge of regret. It would be so lovely to be married to Marc and sit together at night in front of the fire with a glass of wine and perhaps some soft, romantic music.

As if he had read her thoughts, Marc rose to his feet, went across to the cassette deck and put in a tape of one of Jane's favourite musicals. Once the nostalgic notes rippled into the air, Jane sank lower in her seat, closed her eyes and felt a pang of longing go through her. I love you, she thought silently. I love you, Marc. To the end of my life I'll never forget this moment. She felt as if she had never been more vigorously, achingly alive than now, when all her senses tingled with a heightened consciousness. The voices of the singers soared above her, male and female gloriously intertwined; the heat from the fire radiated fiercely on her skin, and the light flared orange through her closed eyelids. She took a deep, slow sip of the port, letting its sweet, sticky potency linger on her tongue, and then swallowed. I wish this moment could last forever, she thought.

Marc was sitting so close that she could smell the spicy scent of his aftershave, feel the way his thigh muscles tensed and hardened when he moved, hear the quiet, deep rhythm of his breathing. Knowing she was being foolish, but powerless to resist, she let her head droop for a moment so that it brushed his shoulder. At once he leaned down and nuzzled her hair, inhaling its fragrance. His left arm came around her shoulders and with a deliberate, unhurried movement he plucked the port glass from her fingers. Jane's eyes flew open. She saw that he had set both glasses on the table and was gazing down at her with an expression that made her heart begin to thud in a frantic, uneven rhythm. The intense, hungry look of need in his face left her in no doubt of what he was about to do as he bent towards her.

'Don't!' she begged in a tormented voice, turning her head aside so that his kiss met her cheek instead of her lips.

'Why not?' he asked lazily, taking her chin in his hand and turning her back to face him. This time his mouth brushed hers in a provocative, fleeting caress that left her quivering and unsatisfied. 'It's what we both want.'

'No,' she gasped. 'N-no... It isn't... I——'

Abruptly his mood seemed to change. Gone was the casual mockery and in its place came an unfamiliar, stormy intensity. With a sudden, swift movement he fell on his knees before her and cupped her face in his hands. His eyes seemed to blaze like molten fire and a muscle in his cheek twitched sharply.

'Tell me you don't want me and I'll go upstairs this moment and never touch you again,' he said in a harsh, urgent voice. 'But for the love of heaven, let me have the truth, Jane! I've wanted you from the moment I first saw you. You're like a fire in my blood, some kind of madness that grips me and won't let me go. And it's the same for you, isn't it? Isn't it? Answer me, woman!'

Jane opened her mouth to protest, to lie, to make some excuse that would keep her safe from the dangerous tide of longing that was engulfing her. He didn't say he loved me, she told herself, only that he wanted me. And he might still be planning to marry Simone... He might... This might only be... a game... a trick... a...

'Well?' he demanded. 'Tell me! Do you want me or not?'

His face was thrust close to hers, so close that she could see the glittering light in his eyes, the twist at the corner of his mouth, could hear the rapid, uneven sound of his breathing. The thought crossed her mind that once she had wondered what it would be like to see Marc Le Rossignol blaze out of control. Well, now she knew. And the smouldering intensity of his gaze demanded nothing less than the truth. Jane caught her breath and shuddered.

'Yes,' she gasped.

A triumphant flame blazed in Marc's eyes and he engulfed her in a hug so fierce that she thought her bones would crack. Then his mouth came down on hers in a long, thrilling kiss that was no longer fleeting, but deep and urgent and wildly arousing. Jane was breathless when at last he released her. His hands gripped her shoulders and he scanned her face as if he was learning every feature by heart.

'You're beautiful,' he said hoarsely. 'Beautiful, wild and passionate. And I'm going to make you mine.'

With a slow, sensual arrogance, as if he was taking possession of her, Marc began to unbutton the silk bodice of her suit. His eyes never left hers for a moment and they were dark, heated, infinitely demanding.

Jane felt as if she were a slave girl being inspected by her new master. Yet, instead of feeling outraged, she found the sensation violently arousing. The truth was that she wanted Marc to take her, dominate her, possess her utterly and claim her as his woman. Waves of moist, pulsating heat throbbed through her as he drew off the silk jacket and flung it indifferently aside. Her bra was a mere wisp of coffee-coloured lace and soon met the same fate. The moment her pink-tipped breasts came into view she felt a wash of colour flood into her cheeks. This far she had travelled already, but not often enough to be calm about it. And beyond this was uncharted territory. Would Marc guess her true inexperience? Even if he didn't, wasn't it crazy to let this happen when she was so unsure of his feelings for her? Crazy or not, I love him! she thought defiantly. He's the only man I've ever loved and I'm willing to take the risk.

Marc flashed her an exultant smile and she smiled back at him, trying to match his recklessness with her own. When he bent his head to her breast and drew her tender, tingling nipple into his mouth she arched her back wantonly, offering herself to him as if she were as expert as himself. But the unfamiliar, tugging caress of his lips sent thrills of excitement through her so intense that she could no longer contain herself. She began to writhe and whimper under his touch and her fingers clutched convulsively at his hair as if she would press him even closer to her.

He was in no hurry, but subjected her other breast to the same delightful torment. By the time he sat back on his heels and looked at her, his eyes dark and strange with desire, she felt as if her whole body were on fire with aching, throbbing need. His deft fingers unzipped her skirt and dropped it to the floor. Then he peeled off her tights and undies and tossed them aside. For the first time in her life Jane had the unsettling experience of being totally naked in front of a man. Her colour came and went, her lips parted and she had to suppress an urge to cross her hands in panic over the silky blonde triangle at the fork of her body.

'Don't be shy,' Marc ordered, running his hand down over her breast and belly and then touching her in the most intimate place of all. 'Relax. You have a beautiful body; you should glory in it. Ah, that's better. Yes, yes. And I can give you greater pleasure than that, *chérie*. Just let me part your legs, so...'

She could not believe what he did next. Of course she had read about things like that in women's magazines—furtively, in doctors' offices, turning back to the decorating page when anybody looked at her—but actually to experience it... Magazines didn't tell you what it felt like to have the man you loved excite you in such an intimate way. Thrill after thrill tingled through her and she began to moan and gasp with incredulous arousal. Unable to believe the sensations that were mounting inside her, she suddenly felt her whole body arch backwards in a stunning climax of satisfied need.

'O-o-o-h!' she gasped, and then slumped forward, shuddering and barely able to breathe.

As she dragged herself into a sitting position Marc pulled her against him, nuzzling her hair and shoulders and letting his hands stray over her body in a slow, caressing rhythm.

'I knew you'd be a passionate, sensual woman,' he whispered in her ear. 'There's some secret wildness that hovers in your eyes like smoke.'

Is there? thought Jane uncertainly. I wish I had more idea of what to do with it, then. If only I could arouse Marc the way he arouses me! I'm so afraid that I'll be a disappointment to him, but if I don't try it soon, I'll lose my nerve. Anyway, it feels strange to have him fully dressed when I'm totally naked. Unable to look him in the face so soon after what he had just done, she turned her head and whispered in his ear.

'Why don't you get undressed too? You're making me feel lonely.'

He gave a soft growl of laughter, deep in the back of his throat.

'All right, my little siren,' he murmured. 'I can't refuse you anything when you ask me in that hoarse, sultry voice. And I certainly don't want you feeling lonely at a moment like this.'

With the grace of a jungle cat he rose to his feet and began to peel off his clothes. Not until that moment had Jane realised just what a magnificent body Marc had. There was not an ounce of spare flesh on him. From his broad shoulders to his narrow hips and powerful legs he was all hard, virile muscle. In the orange glow of the flickering fire Jane thought she had never seen anything so superb as this naked, fully aroused male. Yet what moved her most of all was the way he looked at her.

His eyelids were half closed and his smouldering brown eyes scanned her body with a feverish intensity that terrified and elated her. There was lust in that look, a shameless animal hunger that offered no apologies, but beneath Marc's raw, urgent need she thought she glimpsed something else. A momentary spark of tenderness that transfigured his passion into something glorious. He cares about me, she thought wonderingly, he really cares about me... At least I think he does. Her breath caught in her throat at the realisation and a feeling of wild elation and reck-lessness overwhelmed her. When he stretched out his hand in a sudden, urgent gesture of command, she rose to her feet and glided into his arms like a sleepwalker.

The touch of his warm, muscular body came as a complete shock to her. It felt unfamiliar but won-derful to be hauled against his nakedness, to feel that rough, wiry hair, that heated masculine hardness strained against her. He was so big, so powerful, so demanding that she felt gloriously, intoxicatingly feminine in his embrace. When he buried his face in her neck and nibbled her ear she shuddered with pleasure. That instinctive wriggle of her hips brought a harsh groan from Marc's throat. Closing his eyes, he cupped her soft buttocks in his hands and thrust himself hard against her.

'You drive me wild,' he gasped. 'I've never wanted a woman as I want you. And I'm going to take you until you beg for mercy.'

Just how it happened she didn't know but, a moment later, Jane found herself flat on her back with Marc's weight crushing her satisfyingly into the ticklish sheepskin rug. She thought she would die of pleasure as he braced himself on his elbows and began to explore her body with his tongue. Those nibbling, licking, tantalising kisses were too exquisite and tormenting to be borne and at last, with a groan of protest, she caught her fingers roughly in his hair and drew his head up to hers. He looked at her with a mocking question in his eyes and she kissed him full and fiercely on his open mouth.

Marc had no need of any second invitation. He gave a low growl of triumph deep in the back of his throat, parted her legs with his hand and then drove in. There was a momentary sharp pain of something resisting and tearing that made Jane cry out, then instinct took over. Her body became soft, slick, yielding, welcoming him in as if he had been her lover for years. The rhythmic force of his thrusts had no further power to alarm her and she abandoned herself to a heady, intoxicating surrender.

The room seemed to swirl around her; her eyes closed and she was only dimly aware of the fire's heat, the prickly rug, the drumming of the rain on the roof. All her senses seemed to be focused on the unfamiliar but addictive thrill of what was happening to her. She wound her arms around Marc's neck and clung to him, revelling in the way his hard, masculine strength was driving deep inside her, feeling an anguished delight at the knowledge that the man she loved was taking her for the very first time. It was so special, so momentous that tears sprang to her eyes and she felt a breathless mingling of joy and nostalgia. I wish he knew. I wish I could tell him. I wish it could be as special for him as it is for me, she thought. Then all her feelings suddenly spiralled crazily out of control as an unfamiliar sensation began to build and build inside her like the massing of a tidal wave.

'Marc, I——' she began. And then stopped as the wave suddenly broke, plunging her into a maelstrom of pleasure that made her shudder and cling to him and gasp his name. 'Oh, Marc! Oh, Marc! I love you!'

His breathing quickened, his hold tightened on her; she could feel the frantic thudding of his heart. Then with one final, groaning thrust he too reached his climax and collapsed against her. For a long time there was no sound but their laboured breathing and the hiss and crackle of the log fire with the howling wind and rain as a distant counterpoint.

Marc was still lying on top of Jane, his fingers tangled in her hair, his rough cheek pressed against her smooth one, but she did not complain. In fact, she gloried in the warm, hard mass of his body that was crushing her and making her ache. Would she ever again hold him like this, ever experience such an intimate union once more? Absurdly her eyes began to prickle with tears at the thought and she blinked twice and swallowed, hoping Marc would not notice. A vain hope.

'What's this?' he asked in an appalled voice, raising himself on one elbow and touching one of the drops that was sliding down her cheek. 'You're not crying, are you?'

'N-no,' she choked.

'Jane! What happened? Did I hurt you?'

'No!' she flared. 'Stop interrogating me! I'm fine.'

'Look,' he began, levering himself off her. 'If there's something wrong, you must——'

As he moved he made a discovery. Jane stared back at him in consternation as his eyes slowly rose to meet hers. His face wore a look of mingled pride and exasperation.

'This was your first time, wasn't it?' he asked softly.

She nodded, biting her lip, unable to speak. To her surprise, he bunched her hair on either side of her face and looked down at her searchingly.

'*Chérie*,' he murmured. 'Why didn't you tell me? The first time is so special. I am honoured that you chose me to be the man.'

She had expected him to be hostile, defensive, afraid of being trapped into a commitment he didn't want. His scorn would have been easy to bear—it would have goaded her back into fighting mode, restored her to her tough, aggressive self. But his kindness was more than she could bear. To her horror the tears began to gather faster than ever, blurring her eyes and running down her cheeks.

'I wish you didn't have to go back to France!' she blurted out. Then she covered her face with her arm to hide her stupid, maudlin self-pity.

The hand that drew aside her arm was quite ruthless. Marc's brown eyes gazed down at her with an inscrutable, appraising expression. She glared back at him, hating him for being so aloof, so cool, so untouched by the emotions that were raging through her like a forest fire. Yet his next words took her completely by surprise.

'So,' he said at last. 'If you don't want to be parted from me, then why don't you come to France too?'

CHAPTER SIX

A PAINFUL hope began to flutter deep in Jane's breast. Did this mean that Marc shared her feelings? Could he have fallen in love with her just as she had with him?

'Do you mean . . . that you love me too?' she asked, her eyes kindling.

Marc's features, which had been first indulgent and then calmly appraising, underwent another transformation. His eyes narrowed, his mouth tensed, his expression grew hard and mocking.

'I didn't say that, sweetheart,' he replied caustically. 'I just think it would be a pity if our little affair were to stop when it has barely begun.'

His cruelty cut her to the quick, but at least she no longer felt like crying. Instead she wanted to punch him in the nose. Dashing away the tears, she sat up and wrapped herself into a tight, protective ball with her arms around her knees. How could she have been such a fool as to expose herself to ridicule like that? Her warm, tremulous yearning was suddenly replaced by blazing antagonism. A dangerous expression crossed her face.

'Why would it be a pity?' she asked aggressively.

He shrugged.

'Well, sex improves after the first time.'

'Are you telling me I wasn't any good?' she demanded.

114

'On the contrary, I think you were stupendous. For a beginner.'

'You patronising swine!'

The violence of Jane's emotions astonished her. She hated Marc, she wanted to hit out at him for humiliating her so unbearably. Only moments before she had thought he was sensitive, tender, loving. Now his mood seemed to have changed completely and he seemed bent on transforming an experience of almost mystic beauty into something sordid and ugly. Why? Why was he being so hateful? Were all men like this once they had taken what they wanted?

'There's no need to be crude,' he chided.

'Go to hell! I wouldn't cross the road with you, much less go to France.'

'A pity. We could have a wonderful time together. I could take you to Paris—we could eat dinner in a restaurant overlooking the Seine, visit Notre Dame and the Eiffel Tower, go to some great nightclubs. Then we could drive down through the countryside to Bordeaux. France is very beautiful at this time of the year and we could stop at some of the best vineyards and *caves* on the way.'

'Oh, yes,' retorted Jane with heavy sarcasm. 'And after that?'

'Who knows?' asked Marc, his eyes looking opaque and fathomless. 'There's no point in trying to erect fences around love, or in tying it down to contracts and regulations. That only spoils the magic.'

Jane was silent, biting her lip and trying to come to terms with her own anguish. It was all very well for Marc to talk about 'love', but it was perfectly clear that what he actually meant was sex. Their love-making had left her feeling exalted and transfigured, but after his first brief hint of tenderness Marc now looked like a hunted man on the run. Ready enough for a 'no strings' passion, but deeply uneasy at the thought of being trapped. Obviously he was worried to death that she might want something more serious from him—like a wedding and a lifetime commitment.

'Don't worry. I'm not going to ask you to marry me!' she said scathingly. 'I know you wouldn't have the courage.'

His mouth tightened at that, then his eyes glittered challengingly.

'Just as you wouldn't have the courage to have a love affair with me,' he retorted. 'I thought you had spirit, but it seems I was wrong.'

'It's not a lack of spirit,' flared Jane. 'I just have a healthy measure of self-respect and I don't want to be used by you as if I'm a female on heat and you're my lord and master.'

'Don't you?' taunted Marc. 'I thought that was exactly what you wanted.'

He caught her by the hair and hauled her against him. For an instant she flailed wildly, hissing defiance, then her own treacherous hormones made her succumb. His looming, masculine presence was so arousing that when his arms tightened like steel around her and his tongue thrust urgently between her lips she only gave a faint whimper before surrendering completely.

It was hard to believe that they could both catch fire with such intensity so soon after their previous lovemaking, but within moments their passion was raging out of control as if it fed on the very anger which had ignited it. Yet what had begun so violently soon became tender, exquisite, a complete fusion of body and soul. This time Jane felt only a minor discomfort as Marc slipped inside her and the rhythm of his lovemaking brought her higher and higher to some invisible peak until she soared in ecstasy again.

She had thought she hated him, but she lay beside him, clutching him as if she could never bear to let him go. At last he raised himself on one elbow, trailed his forefinger down between her breasts and looked at her with an odd, bitter smile.

'I'm sorry for what I said to you before,' he announced abruptly. 'You wake the strangest emotions in me, Jane—some of them extremely destructive. But I do want you to come to France with me. Will you?'

Jane stared at him in bewilderment. As an apology it was totally unsatisfactory, because it explained nothing. Marc didn't even sound particularly sorry. He sounded angry and resentful about the feelings she aroused in him, whatever they were. She would be a fool to accept such an ungracious, cryptic invitation and yet... I can't bear to let him go, she thought. I know it's madness, but at least he'll be mine for a few more months. Or weeks. Or days. Until he tires of me.

'Will you?' he repeated.

'Yes,' she said resentfully.

A week later Jane stood outside the front door of Saddler's Corner, giving Brett a key and a final list of instructions.

'Charlie will take care of the winery and the vineyard,' she said. 'But if you could just keep an eye on the house and watch out for vandals I'd be grateful.'

'No worries,' agreed Brett. 'You've left phone numbers where I can contact you, haven't you?'

'It's all written down on the itinerary.'

'When do you reckon you'll be back?'

A fleeting array of emotions crossed Jane's face. Hope, despair, confusion.

'I don't know,' she admitted.

'It must be serious, then,' said Brett. 'I never would have thought it of that Frenchie, but good luck to you, mate. It all turned out for the best really, didn't it? You and Marc, me and Karen. Things are looking pretty serious for us too, just quietly.'

'I'm so pleased!' exclaimed Jane sincerely, standing on her toes to peck Brett on the cheek. 'She's a lovely girl. I hope I'll see you married one of these days.'

'Yeah, likewise,' beamed Brett.

Jane gritted her teeth so hard that they hurt in order not to reveal any of her true feelings on the subject of marriage. Marc had made it abundantly clear that marriage wasn't what he had in mind, but she knew Brett's loyalty and decency well enough not to want an outright fight between the two men. After all, she had made her choice and would have to live with the consequences of it. In spite of the pain it caused her, she had decided that she wanted Marc Le Rossignol at any cost, even if that meant denying her longing for a husband and family of her own. What was more, she intended to enjoy the relationship as long as it lasted, even though she had to admit to herself that there was a defiant, feverish tone to her enjoyment. Even if Marc dropped her once this trip was over, she meant to make the most of every precious moment that remained.

Oddly enough, she succeeded—at least for a while. They travelled via America and she spent an unforgettable evening at a Hawaiian luau, eating vast quantities of barbecued pig and tropical fruit before learning to dance the hula on a moonlit, palm-fringed beach with Marc laughing and toasting her efforts. Then there was a magical weekend in New York with a suite overlooking the lights of Manhattan. And after that Paris, a city made for lovers. Jane cherished each day as if it were a jewel that could never be robbed from her once she had taken possession of it.

Her frenzied gaiety sustained her all the way until they reached Bordeaux. As they drove through the beautiful country of the Gironde estuary her spirits plummeted abruptly. It was no use! While they were jetsetting from continent to continent it had been easy enough for Jane to pretend that she was pleasure-seeking and sophisticated, but seeing this place brought her down to earth with a jolt. This was real! Marc had spent most of his youth and manhood here, his family and friends were here and she realised now that she wanted desperately to be accepted by them, to become a part of their lives.

How had she ever convinced herself that she could stay light-hearted and smiling when the time came for them to part? She didn't want to part from Marc! She wanted to belong with him, now and forever. What a hollow mockery this trip was turning out to be! And how differently she would have felt about it if it had been genuine. If only he were bringing her home proudly to meet his family and friends before announcing their forthcoming wedding, how thrilled she would feel. Instead she felt with each passing kilometre that she was an intruder who didn't belong here.

A small, stark smile touched her lips as she looked out at the honey-coloured buildings with their tiled roofs and green shutters, the countryside so neat and orderly with its profusion of trees and rows of vines, its geraniums spilling from windowsills. When they stopped for lunch at a small restaurant attached to one of the *caves*, Jane was silent and preoccupied, although she was storing away every detail in her memory so that she could draw it all out later and reflect upon it—the sound of birdsong in the trees, the distant roar of motorcycles on the road, the echo of the proprietor's footsteps as he led them down the cool, winding staircase to the underground cellar where they sampled some of the wines. Then there was the courtyard itself, with water splashing into an ancient stone basin from a lion-headed fountain and Marc smiling at her across a table laden with chicken-liver pâté and crusty bread and quiche and salad, while all the time her misery was building and building until it threatened to choke her.

'You're very quiet,' commented Marc as they got back into the car to continue their journey. 'Is something wrong?'

'Are you sure your parents won't mind my just arriving like this?' she burst out.

He shrugged.

'I told them you were coming. Why should they mind?'

'Because it's a long way from Australia to France,' she said unsteadily. 'It's not the sort of trip you make just to have a cup of coffee. Won't they think——?'

She broke off, but the words hovered, bitter and unspoken, inside her head. Won't they think there's something serious going on between us? Surely Marc's parents were entitled to think such a thing when he had brought Jane such a great distance to stay with them? Surely she was entitled to think it herself? She tossed her head restlessly, sending her mane of tumbling curly hair swirling around her shoulders, as if she could shake off her thoughts. Marc simply glanced at her quizzically, content to let her flounder without offering any help. At last she was driven to ask him a question outright.

'What did you tell them about me?' she asked in a tormented voice.

'Just that you were a friend who was coming to stay.'

'Oh,' muttered Jane with a touch of disappointment.

'And that we're sleeping together and want to share a room.'

Jane practically swallowed her tongue.

'Oh, Marc!' she wailed. 'You didn't! I'll be too embarrassed to look them in the face. What on earth will they think of me?'

He raised his eyes as if she was making a great fuss about nothing.

'That you're a grown woman who enjoys the pleasures of life,' he retorted. 'What's wrong with that?'

Everything, thought Jane bitterly, clamping her lower lip between her teeth and staring out of the window. I don't just go to bed with you because it's one of the great pleasures of life, even though it is, but because I love you! Yet she had already made a fool of herself once by revealing her feelings to Marc and was determined never to do it again. She shrugged.

'Nothing,' she said coolly.

'Do that again,' he ordered.

'What?' she demanded in a mystified voice.

'The shrug. You were amazing—you looked so typically French. You must be a natural mimic.'

'Tell me,' said Jane sweetly. 'Is there a typically French way of punching someone in the nose? If so, I'd like to put my natural mimicry to work and learn it.'

'You're annoyed with me about something, aren't you?' asked Marc.

'How very perceptive of you,' said Jane. 'I am.'

'What's wrong?'

'Why don't you put all that French intuition to work and figure it out, *chéri*?'

After that they drove in silence until they had almost reached Cadillac, although Marc kept casting Jane occasional long, scrutinising glances.

Jane herself was busy trying to control the ferment of her feelings. All this cynicism didn't come naturally to her and she had the ominous suspicion that the bottling up of her emotions was soon going to lead to a violent outburst. She realised now that she resented the way that she had been lured into this relationship purely on Marc's terms. It was all very well to pretend that she wanted to be as sophisticated and shallow as he was, but she didn't! She wanted a deep, passionate, tempestuous commitment for life. Love and marriage, nothing less. But she was not likely to get it unless Marc changed dramatically. She glanced sharply across at him and he scowled and looked away. Perhaps he *will* change dramatically, she thought, without much hope. Perhaps I'll get on so well with his parents and friends that he'll realise we belong together for life. Her thoughts skimmed away into a soft-focused daydream where Marc's mother was singing her praises for learning to cook such magnificent *crème brûlée*—this was difficult to believe, really, since Jane's cooking was of the burnt scrambled egg variety, and scrambled egg *brûlée* just didn't have the same ring. Suddenly Marc turned into a side road.

'We're here,' he announced.

Jane looked up with a start and saw an ornate iron gateway set into a mellow gold stucco wall festooned with Virginia creeper which formed the entrance to a huge château. Even then she didn't guess the truth.

'What's this, another winery?' she asked. 'Are you going to buy a bottle to take home to your parents?'

'Not exactly,' said Marc, his lips twitching. 'This is my home and my parents should be inside the house somewhere.'

Jane gasped. The building in front of them looked large enough to house an army. Through the open gateway she could see a vast gravel courtyard. Around it, forming three sides of a square, sprawled an elegant eighteenth-century château. Beyond the main building at the far side of the courtyard rose turrets belonging to an even older era. The sort of turrets that Jane remembered from her childhood copy of *Cinderella*.

'I thought you said your home was old and shabby,' she murmured, aghast.

'It is,' agreed Marc carelessly. 'The oldest section belongs to the fourteenth century and some of the furniture even in the newer part is really knocked about. Especially the Louis XIV cabinets.'

'Louis XIV?' echoed Jane faintly. 'Wasn't he alive in the seventeenth century?'

'That's right,' said Marc. 'But don't let it worry you. It's a big château, with a lot of old and beautiful things in it, but we live quite a casual life in many ways.'

Jane couldn't imagine anything less casual than the entrance hall of the château or the people who came to meet them. There was a tall woman with aristocratic features and iron-grey hair whose dark, penetrating eyes and sphinx-like smile reminded Jane of Marc in a particularly difficult mood. And beside her stood a twinkling blue-eyed man, an inch or two shorter than his wife, who was full of charm and warmth. Both of them were exquisitely dressed in anything but a casual manner. Marc's mother wore a white silk blouse, red tailored suit, gold earrings and gold necklace, and high-heeled shoes, while her grey hair was stylishly permed. His father was equally smart in a charcoal-grey suit, striped shirt, and blue and charcoal tie. As they advanced towards her Jane suppressed an impulse to curtsy or run back to the car to comb her hair.

'Jane, I'd like you to meet my parents. Monsieur and Madame Le Rossignol.'

'*Enchantée,*' murmured Jane.

She found herself enveloped in a cloud of Arpège as Marc's mother kissed her on both cheeks. In spite of the friendly gesture, she sensed a certain reserve in the older woman's manner and felt that the shrewd brown eyes were darting over her, missing nothing. Marc's father was far more welcoming. He hugged Jane with unmistakable warmth and held her at arm's length to appraise her.

'You are a very beautiful young lady, Mademoiselle West,' he said with an approving nod. 'And one who will improve with age. It is clear that my son has a connoisseur's taste.'

Jane's clear, rippling laugh rang out.

'You make me sound like a vintage wine,' she protested, her eyes dancing. 'But thank you, *monsieur*. And please, call me Jane. Mademoiselle West sounds so formal.'

Both Marc's parents looked taken aback at this invitation, so that Jane wondered uneasily whether she had made a *faux pas*.

'Australians are very informal,' Marc explained hastily. 'In Australia it's common for adults to be on first-name terms immediately they meet. It's a sign of friendly intentions.'

'Ah, *bon*,' agreed Monsieur Le Rossignol. 'In that case, Jane, you must call us Armand and Yvonne.'

Marc's mother looked less than enthralled at this invitation, but she gave Jane a small, tight smile which did not reach her eyes.

'My husband is right . . . Jane,' she said heroically. 'Please call us by our Christian names if that is your custom. Now, let me show you to your rooms and then we can all meet for a glass of wine in the garden.'

'There's no need for that, Maman,' protested Marc. 'I can show Jane the way.'

'She's my guest, Marc. I must see that she has everything she needs.'

Miserably Jane followed as Yvonne led the way out of the eighteenth-century building into the older part of the château. She felt gauche and uneasy, as if she had done the wrong thing from the very beginning, and she grew even more uncomfortable when Yvonne showed them into a suite of rooms at the top of one of the old towers. The view from the small window was breathtaking, looking as it did over miles and miles of vineyards and woods and rustic farmhouses, but Jane had eyes for only one thing. The vast, six-teenth-century bed which dominated the room and which seemed to her overheated imagination like a defiant symbol of her illicit relationship with Marc.

What did Yvonne Le Rossignol think of Jane for conducting an affair with her son so brazenly beneath her own roof? Did she resent her and wish she would leave? Was she secretly shocked? Would she protest heatedly over the matter to Marc when Jane was out of the way? Whatever the true answers were to these questions, Yvonne gave no hint of her feelings as she turned down the coverlet on the massive bed and ges-tured to a bedside cupboard laden with flowers, tissues and books, and a carafe of water.

'I hope you find everything you need, Jane,' she said briskly. 'I'm afraid the bathroom is on the next floor down, which one must admit is inconvenient, but Marc thought you would like the romantic at-mosphere of the old château. Gaston will be up soon with your luggage and there's a bellpull on the wall which rings in the kitchen. If you need anything else you can pull that, but do be patient. Our housekeeper is elderly and she's slow on the stairs.'

Jane immediately felt as if she were a heartless in-truder who had only come to France for the purpose of torturing old women with bunions. She gave Marc's mother a troubled smile.

'Thank you,' she murmured. 'You're very kind.'

Then she decided to try out her French as a goodwill gesture.

'*Vous êtes trés gentille, madame.*'

'*Je vous en prie, mademoiselle,*' replied Yvonne smoothly and then withdrew.

'She doesn't like me!' burst out Jane, the moment the echo of footsteps on the stone stairs had died away.

'Don't be ridiculous,' retorted Marc. 'Give her time.'

'She called me "*vous*". That's the unfriendly form of you, isn't it?'

'Not necessarily! She was being polite, that's all. She belongs to the old school and her manners are more formal than yours. Anyway, my father likes you.'

'Maybe,' muttered Jane sceptically. 'But he might be only pretending.'

'What's this all about?' asked Marc, taking her in his arms and kissing her thoroughly. 'You don't normally suffer from shyness.'

In spite of his disarming words, he didn't seem very interested in her answer. He began nibbling her ear in a manner which normally sent quivers of excitement thrilling through her body, but this time she jerked her head away and glared at him.

'I don't normally feel like an outsider!' she said. 'But I do here. I'm a foreigner and I don't know the right thing to do. It makes me feel confused and out of place, as if I don't belong.'

'You'll soon fit in,' Marc assured her carelessly. 'Besides, you've got me to cling to. I'll guide you.'

Jane sat down on the bed with an exasperated sigh.

'I'm not the clinging type,' she retorted stormily.

Even as she said it she was no longer sure it was true. Once she had prided herself on her independence, but now she was so deeply in love with Marc that it felt as if she were sinking in quicksand. What annoyed her most was that she did have a powerful, instinctive urge to cling to him and count on him to guide her. If matters had been different, she might have done so. Yet as she gazed tempestuously up at him she realised that Marc himself was the cause of most of her insecurity. If only he hadn't insisted that they share a room, she wouldn't have felt so uncomfortable about being scrutinised by his mother. Or if they had come here as an engaged couple, she could have faced the ordeal with more poise. What upset her and made her feel vulnerable was the indignity and uncertainty of her position.

'Don't you like it here?' asked Marc abruptly.

'I don't know,' muttered Jane with an ungracious shrug.

He made one more attempt to overcome her ill-humour. Crouching on the floor in front of her, he put his arms around her and buried his face in her hair, but she thrust him away impatiently.

'Shouldn't we go down?' she demanded in a brittle voice. 'Your parents will be expecting us, won't they?'

With a sigh Marc rose to his feet and led the way in silence. They found a table laid in the shadow of a tree in the walled garden at the foot of the tower. Jane produced the presents she had brought from Australia—a tie for Marc's father and an opal brooch for his mother—and there were exclamations of surprise and delight. Armand insisted on changing his tie immediately in order to wear the new one, and even Marc's mother seemed to thaw considerably as she asked Jane to pin the brooch on the lapel of her jacket.

'Thank you, my dear. It's magnificent.'

Armand began busily opening bottles of wine and mineral water, while urging them both to sit down.

'What will you have, Jane?' he asked. 'A white or a red?'

'A red, please.'

'Tell him what you think of it, Jane,' urged Marc with a note of pride in his voice as she accepted a glass of Cabernet Sauvignon.

Gaining confidence from the reaction to her gifts, Jane sniffed, swirled and sipped thoughtfully.

'It's excellent. It has a rich colour, a light tobacco aroma and a hint of red berry scent with a very dense, vigorous flavour.'

'Ah, she has the palate, this little one!' exclaimed Armand in delight. 'You have been training her, Marc.'

'No. She was already very knowledgeable when I met her. She's a professional winemaker herself.'

'*Formidable*! Then we should leave this table and do some serious tasting in the cellar, isn't that so? What do you say, Mademoiselle Jane?'

Jane glanced enquiringly at Marc's mother, who flung up her hands in despair.

'Go, go!' she urged. 'Jane, you will soon realise that the men in this family have red wine in their veins in the place of red blood. If you can talk knowledgeably about wines you will win their hearts, but don't let them bore you. I'll see you again at dinnertime.'

Marc and Jane spent an enjoyable two hours in the cellar and the vineyard while Armand initiated his guest into the mysteries of the '*terroir*'—that indescribable combination of soil and climate and other factors that gave each wine its own individual quality. He grew positively lyrical as he talked about gravelly hilltops and northern exposures, about *burriques* and pruning and the use of egg-whites to clarify new wine. Marc watched with a look of amusement and approval as Jane and his father sipped and compared and argued. Shortly after five o'clock Armand glanced at his watch and gave a guilty start.

'*Mon Dieu*! I offer you a thousand apologies, Jane! I enjoy myself so much that I forget the time. I did not mean to keep you so long.'

'I've enjoyed it too,' said Jane sincerely.

'*Bon*,' beamed Armand. 'Then tomorrow we continue. I'll show you where I tore out the old vines that weren't producing and fumigated the ground with mustard gas before replacing them. Ah, what an outcry there was from the traditionalists! But you should see what an improved yield we have now!'

Jane's eyes twinkled as her gaze met Marc's over his father's shoulder, although she did not reveal that she knew who had really been responsible for the innovation.

'You must be very pleased with your decision,' she said diplomatically.

'Yes, yes,' he agreed. 'And do you know what I always say to my critics now? I say, tradition is a fine thing, but we must have innovation too! And that's where you Australians can show us the way. From what my son tells me, you are great innovators in the field of winemaking. Well, that's what we need—a marriage of the old world and the new.'

He beamed fondly at both of them, and a sudden gleam came into his eyes as if he had just become conscious of a double meaning in his own words.

'A marriage of the old world with the new,' he repeated, chuckling softly to himself. 'Yes, indeed, that may be exactly what we need.'

His gaze met Jane's with a look of humorous complicity, as if expecting that she might spring a sudden exciting announcement on him. If she had really come here as a prospective daughter-in-law, Jane would have been touched by Armand's evident support for her cause. As it was, his broad hint threw her into confusion and she looked helplessly at Marc, half longing for him to confirm his father's suspicions. Instead Marc's features twisted into an expression of weary, sardonic exasperation. Armand gave a faint sigh and shook his head.

'Well, *mes enfants*, it's getting late and I mustn't delay you any longer,' he said in a disappointed voice. 'Take Jane upstairs to repose herself, Marc, and we will see you later at dinner.'

Once the door of their bedroom in the tower had closed securely behind them, Marc took Jane in his arms and smiled wryly down at her.

'I'm sorry about my father's rather heavy-handed matchmaking attempts,' he said. 'He's always wanted me to marry and he doesn't seem to accept that not everybody regards marriage as a passport to eternal bliss.'

'Don't apologise,' retorted Jane coldly, hating Marc for his cynicism. 'I think your father's a sweetie.'

'Well, you've certainly made a conquest of him.'

'Perhaps, but I don't think your mother will ever accept me,' she said, breaking away from him.

'Does it really matter?' he asked. 'The chances are that you won't be staying here long, and you may never come back again.'

'Thanks. It's interesting to know that I've worn my welcome out so quickly.'

'Did I say that?' demanded Marc fiercely.

He caught her arm as she paced restlessly past him and hauled her into his arms with a turbulence that alarmed and enthralled her. Before she knew what was happening she was kissing him back with all the impetuous force of her mingled anger and love and hatred. It was a potent brew and Marc caught his breath and began to unbutton her dress with urgent, wrenching movements. Soon they were rolling together on the vast bed, panting and gasping and kissing with a frenzy born of violent mutual need.

Jane surrendered herself to him with total abandon, but her physical wildness could not be matched by an equal emotional surrender. Although she was aching with love, bewilderment and despair, she dared not reveal any of this to Marc. Instead it had to remain a poignant secret that left a haunted look in her eyes and a wistful smile hovering around the corners of her lips even after he had brought her to the heights of ecstasy. Long after their breathing had slowed, when they were still lying exhausted together, Marc raised himself on one elbow and lay gazing down at her in the half-light from the tiny window.

'Your eyes are full of secrets,' he complained as he caressed her face with his fingertips. 'I never know what you're thinking.'

'I'm thinking how terrible it is to want something really badly and fear that you'll never be able to get it,' she admitted huskily.

A brooding look came into his face and he seemed on the point of saying something, but then frowned and fell silent. Rising to his feet, he crossed to the window and stood with one arm flung up against the architrave, gazing moodily out at the countryside beneath. When at last he did speak, his words surprised her.

'I suppose you're thinking of your vineyard in Tasmania,' he said over his shoulder.

No, I was thinking of you, Jane wanted to exclaim, but the words faltered on her lips and remained unspoken. To her astonishment she realised that she had scarcely given a thought to her vineyard ever since they had left Tasmania. All she had thought of was Marc. Yet she could hardly tell him that when he was so remote, so aloof, so intent on reminding her that she had no permanent place here in his home. So insistent that any suggestion of marriage between them was utterly ridiculous.

'Yes, I am,' she lied, and her mouth hardened.

Marc swung around and gazed at her with an intent, piercing scrutiny.

'It must mean a lot to you,' he said with a touch of bitterness.

'It means everything to me!' she flashed. She could hear the passion and anger and love vibrating in her own voice, and could only hope that Marc would believe it was her vineyard that she cared about so intensely.

'I see,' he muttered, and for a brief moment he was himself again. Calm, detached, indifferent. 'Well, I'm sure we can work something out. I'm not an ogre. I don't want to deprive you of what's rightfully yours.'

'Don't you?' she challenged. 'That's nice of you. But it all comes back to a rather difficult question, doesn't it? What is rightfully mine?'

The light was fading fast, so that she could no longer see his features clearly. Against the rectangle of silvery sky he looked dark, ominous, threatening—every inch the unwelcome invader she had once considered him. Her heart began to thud unevenly, so that she felt she would suffocate from her burden of mingled hate and love. She knew perfectly well what she considered rightfully hers. Marc Le Rossignol as her husband, lover and the father of her children, to stand by her for the rest of her life. But that was the one right he would never concede her. In the gathering gloom she thought she saw his lips curl in a sardonic line.

'You're in a strange mood,' he pointed out. 'You've been acting oddly ever since we arrived here.'

She vowed to match his coolness with her own. Although she was almost shaking with the intensity of her feelings, she forced herself to appear composed.

'Have I?' she demanded blandly, rising to her feet and beginning to reach for her clothes. 'Well, why not? Changeability is a woman's privilege, isn't it?'

'It certainly seems to be yours, at any rate,' he growled resentfully. 'You came on this trip of your own free will and you seemed to be enjoying yourself in America and Paris. Now, ever since we've arrived here, you seem to be on thorns... No, what do you say? Like a cat on hot bricks! Why? What's the matter with you?'

Jane hunched one shoulder and smiled bitterly, fastening her dress with swift, angry movements.

'Guess,' she invited.

Marc swore under his breath. Unlike her, he did not bother to hurry into his clothes, but seemed quite indifferent to his own nakedness.

Darting a covert glance at that savage, virile body, Jane wished she could remain so easily indifferent. His presence was a torment to her, a reminder of an intense physical intimacy that was unmatched by any corresponding emotional union. In that moment they seemed so distant from each other that they might have been total strangers or even sworn enemies. Had she really given herself to a man who was never going to let her cross the threshold of his heart? The thought wounded her so deeply that her eyes blazed with hostility.

'Is it possible that you're tired of me so soon?' he drawled insultingly. 'There's no need for this little amour to continue, you know, if it no longer amuses you. We can part whenever you wish.'

'Just as you like!' flared Jane. 'We don't want it to become tedious, do we?'

Her throat felt so raw and scraped that she could barely swallow, and hot, stinging tears rose threateningly in her eyes. Had they really descended to this point, and so soon? Well, she couldn't say Simone hadn't warned her! Obviously Marc had been only amusing himself with her and was now looking for a way of giving her the brush-off. She caught her upper lip between her teeth and fought to control herself.

'So you're bored, are you?' asked Marc in a conversational tone. '*Ma foi*! That didn't take long.'

'I'm not bored!' burst out Jane, too distraught for further subterfuge. 'I'm upset and I'm confused. It may all be a big joke to you, but I don't go around just having affairs for the fun of it. When your father talks as if he's expecting us to marry, it makes me feel cornered. It makes me feel... Oh, I can't... It... We...'

Her voice trailed off as she found herself quite unable to say what she meant in the face of Marc's unnervingly silent gaze. With a disconcerting suddenness he drew the curtains and snapped on a lamp-switch so that a soft, peach-like glow lit the room.

'What do you want to do about it?' he asked levelly.

I want to marry you, she thought, but pride would not let her utter the words. Not when he was standing there gazing at her with that mocking lift to his eyebrows and that cruel smile flickering around the edges of his mouth. Desperately she sought for some way to gain a hint of his intentions, some sign that his feelings were engaged and not merely his sexual appetite. If he planned to return to Australia, wouldn't that mean that she had at least some hope of developing a real relationship with him?

'What are you going to do about my father's property?' she asked abruptly. 'Do you still intend to buy it and manage it yourself?'

'I don't know!' he snapped, his eyes glittering. 'Frankly it's not a question of major importance to me any longer. On the whole, I very much doubt it.'

A shudder went through her and she closed her eyes briefly, as if a knife had just pierced her flesh. So she might never see him again once this French trip was over. How would she ever bear it?

'I see,' she said shakily. 'Look, Marc, you asked me what I wanted to do. Well, I'll tell you. This affair we're having is more than I can handle. I want to stop sleeping with you.'

If she had hoped he would argue with her, demand explanations, drag her into a tempestuous quarrel which would clear the air, she was disappointed. He simply shrugged and began to pull on his clothes.

'Just as you like. As a matter of courtesy to my parents, I hope you'll stay another week or two to see the region before you return to Australia. There's a spare bedroom at the foot of the tower. I'll move your things down there tonight.'

'Won't your mother think——?' began Jane in a tormented voice.

'She'll think nothing!' he snapped. 'There's no need for her even to know about it.'

Jane winced as Marc finished dressing with an ominous scowl on his face.

They went down to dinner in a highly charged, hostile silence. This was a pity, really, since Marc's mother had clearly gone to a good deal of trouble over the meal. The heavy mahogany table was covered in a starched white double damask tablecloth, with a vase full of orange lilies in the centre and a setting of fine china, crystal wine glasses and heavy silver cutlery, all illuminated by flickering candlelight. Faced with such a welcome, Jane did her best to be an agreeable companion and was soon deep in conversation with Marc's father about her recent six-month stay in the Champagne country.

The food was very good. Scallops in a cream sauce followed by a casserole of beef with olives and tomatoes served with pasta, and a lemon mousse for dessert. What had begun as mere good manners soon became a genuine pleasure as Jane discovered an unexpected link with Marc's mother in the form of a shared interest in collecting old lace. They were deep in a discussion of lacemaking techniques by the time Marie brought in the coffee and Jane's mercurial spirits were beginning to rise again. Perhaps she would be accepted here—perhaps both Marc's parents would grow fond of her. And, when he saw how well she fitted in with his family, perhaps he would begin to reconsider his opposition to marriage. She flashed him a hesitant peacemaking smile across the vase of lilies, but he merely frowned in reply.

'Oh, Marc,' said his mother, interrupting this silent byplay. 'I want you to keep tomorrow free. I've invited the whole family for lunch so that they can all meet Jane.'

'That's nice,' replied Marc without much interest.

'And there's something else, *chéri*. Simone telephoned this afternoon to find out when we were expecting you and I told her you were already here. She said she had some matters of great importance to discuss with you, so I've invited her to stay for a few days.'

CHAPTER SEVEN

JANE dropped her coffee-cup into her saucer with a clatter. As if things weren't bad enough between her and Marc, now she was going to have Simone here, gloating over her discomfiture! But surely Marc wouldn't allow it? Surely he would make some protest, take some defensive action to keep the two of them apart? After what had happened between him and Jane in recent weeks he couldn't possibly want to throw the two women together...could he? To her dismay Marc merely raised his eyebrows slightly at his mother's announcement, gave a thoughtful half-smile and nodded.

'Good,' he said. 'I intended to track Simone down. This will save me the trouble of pursuing her.'

Jane could scarcely contain her outrage at this bland statement. When Marc's father suggested a game of cards she pleaded a headache that was rapidly becoming genuine and escaped to the oldest part of the château. Marc caught her up in the tower room as she was busy cramming her clothes into her suitcase, with her lips set in a thin line and a stormy expression in her green eyes.

'Do you still want to desert me, then?' he asked in a mild tone.

She cast him a burning look.

'Yes,' she said shortly.

As a matter of fact, she was by no means as sure of her decision as she sounded. When she had first

heard of Simone's imminent arrival a crazy impulse
had seized her to alter her decision about deserting
Marc's bed. A primitive urge to cling to her man and
fight off any rival females. Yet a brief reflection had
shown her how ridiculous that was. If Marc didn't
care about her enough to try and persuade her to stay
or to make any genuine commitment to her, then
sharing a bed with him was hardly likely to make any
difference! No doubt if Simone was coming to the
château with the express purpose of seducing him, she
would soon persuade Marc to get rid of Jane without
any difficulty at all! No, it was much better to preserve her pride and end their love affair by her own
choice. Flashing him another look full of loathing,
Jane did up the clasps on her suitcase with shaking
fingers.

'Is everything ready to go, then?' he asked.

She could have hit him.

'Is that all you're going to say?' she flared.

'What else is there to say?' he demanded mockingly. 'Should I tell you that I'm desolated at your
desertion? That you've wounded me beyond
measure?'

'Oh, shut up!' snapped Jane, unable to bear any
more.

As Marc carried the two heavy suitcases effortlessly
down the spiral staircase Jane was uneasily conscious
of the oppressive atmosphere between them. He was
almost insultingly calm about the whole episode, but
she thought she saw something dangerous flash in his
eyes as he set her bags down on the floor of the spare
bedroom. A heady feeling of anticipation swept over
her and she wondered if they were on the brink of a
confrontation which would strip aside all their polite

pretences and lay bare their true feelings for each other. It was almost a disappointment when Marc wished her goodnight with a cool nod.

Left alone, she locked the door as if she were in some danger of attack and then undressed impetuously, flinging her clothes all over the floor in a way that would have made Marc shudder. Then the realisation that Marc would no longer know or care how untidy she was sent an odd twinge that was close to pain through her. Even the simple task of pulling on her nightdress was a reminder of how much life had changed since she had met him. In the past she had worn tatty old cotton pyjamas, but this frothy confection of pale green charmeuse satin with a cream lace jacket had been bought purely for the purpose of dazzling Marc. It seemed a pathetic irony that she should now be wearing it as she huddled alone in the centre of a vast antique French bed. A room like this would be wonderful for lovers, but was overwhelming and rather spooky for someone on her own.

It's going to be awfully lonely without him, thought Jane with a sinking feeling. Oh, don't be such a wimp! she told herself crossly. Lots of women break off affairs with men they love, and they don't all fall to pieces once they're alone.

Men they love... The phrase echoed in her head, making her flinch. Yes, that was the trouble. She did still love Marc, so why had she insisted on this separation, when it wasn't what she really wanted at all? Even now she could still creep up the stairs to Marc's room and find herself tumbled across his bed in a display of passion that would have her gasping; she knew that without a doubt. But in the morning nothing would be changed, she told herself bitterly.

I still wouldn't know whether he cares about me or whether it's all just some kind of combat sport to him. It's better to keep what's left of my pride and refuse to sleep with him any more.

A small nagging voice inside her head told her that if she really had any pride she would leave the château completely and never see Marc again. Oh, no, I couldn't! she protested at once. It would offend Marc's parents. Yet deep down she knew that this was only an excuse. The truth was that she craved his company so desperately that she wasn't strong enough to give him up. It was like being hooked on some addictive drug which she could only relinquish slowly, with a constant danger of relapse ... And it would be worse once Simone arrived. How on earth could she bear to see him with the other woman?

Surprisingly it was less of an ordeal than she expected to confront Marc the following morning. Shortly after seven o'clock there was a tap on her bedroom door.

'Come in!' yawned Jane, sitting up and pushing her hair out of her eyes.

The massive oak door swung open with a creak and there stood Marc, already dressed and posed like a waiter on stage with a circular tray uplifted on the palm of his right hand.

'What in the world——?' began Jane.

'A peace offering,' explained Marc, transferring the tray to waist level with a flourish and then setting it on her lap. 'I thought we might have coffee and croissants and then go for a walk together. It's time you saw some of the local countryside—if you're going to stay?'

There was just a hint of a question in the last phrase and Jane felt her cheeks grow warm as Marc watched her steadily. Unable to meet his eyes, she gave a small, shamefaced nod.

'Yes, I am going to stay,' she replied in a rush. 'But I'm not going to share a room with you, Marc. I just feel——'

His fingers touched her lips, halting her disjointed explanation before it really began.

'You don't have to explain,' he told her carelessly. 'There are plenty of other pleasures we can share. Sightseeing, dining out, shopping...'

Jane sighed faintly as she took her first sip of hot, dense black coffee. Somehow Marc managed to put their lovemaking on the same level as any other enjoyable pastime. Was that all it meant to him? She didn't dare to ask for fear of straying into a minefield where she would feel dangerously vulnerable.

'I suppose so,' she agreed, striving to match his careless mood. 'Do you have any plans, then?'

Marc bit into a pastry covered with currants and a sweet glaze and nodded.

'Mmm. My parents never surface on Sunday mornings, so I thought that you and I might walk into the village of St Sulpice, have a look round and then come back in time for this wretched family lunch at one o'clock.'

Half an hour later Marc and Jane paused on the path leading towards the village to look back at the château, sitting solidly on a carpet of vivid green grass with symmetrical rows of vines surrounding it in all directions. The bright morning sun glinted off the steep, tiled roofs and sent long shadows plummeting down from the clipped box shrubs that bordered the terrace. Beyond the turreted part of the building, the eighteenth-century addition was just visible behind a clump of assorted trees—silver birch, ash, elms and a couple of pine trees.

'It's an amazing place, isn't it?' said Jane, shading her eyes. 'Almost like two completely different separate homes, just joined together by that connecting hall.'

'That's exactly what it is,' agreed Marc. 'According to family tradition, one of my ancestors in the eighteenth century wanted to marry a certain girl, but she didn't like the old château. She complained that it was dark and poky and inconvenient, so he spent more than half his fortune building a new house to please her.'

'Oh, how gorgeous!' cried Jane. 'What a nice man he must have been. Would you do that if you really loved someone and wanted to marry her?'

'No,' said Marc shortly. 'I think women are quite unreasonable enough as it is without any encouragement from men.'

Jane pulled a face.

'You don't really like women much, do you?' she demanded accusingly.

Marc smiled with that lazy, sardonic twist to his lips that always made her long to hit him.

'They're all very well in their place,' he replied in a bored tone. 'But a man would be a fool to let them have the upper hand. Or to rearrange his life to please them. I never would.'

During the remaining two-mile walk to St Sulpice Jane eyed her companion with exasperation. Sometimes she felt tantalisingly close to understanding just what made Marc Le Rossignol tick, but his maddening refusal to allow any genuine emotional intimacy always cut her off short. All the same, she had a strong suspicion that some woman had once hurt him very badly, leaving him permanently embittered against all others. If that was true, would she ever manage to break through his sophisticated nonchalance and win some kind of emotional response? And where did Simone fit in with all this? Could she really be content to let him have affairs with other women, when he was planning to marry her? But was he planning to marry Simone? Or was that just a blatant lie that she had told to scare Jane off? It made Jane's head ache even to think about it. I ought to have the courage to ask him straight out, she thought. Yet pride and embarrassment kept her silent.

Fortunately Marc diverted her thoughts by pointing out landmarks as they walked. The elm trees which he had climbed as a boy, the stream where he had fished with his brothers, an old, ruined chapel which made him halt and chuckle reminiscently.

'I took my younger sister out there one night after we'd been fishing,' he recalled. 'I told her it was haunted and then pretended I could hear groans coming from inside. When I asked her to go and investigate with me she practically had hysterics from terror. Little idiot! Of course, it was rather spooky at midnight.'

The chapel looked peaceful enough now, drowsing in the golden morning sunlight with its steep roof fallen in and the scattered rubble overgrown with vegetation so that it looked like a wrecked ship about to vanish beneath a sea of green vines. Yet Jane could see how it might well appear eerie if seen by moonlight.

'How could you be so mean?' she demanded indignantly.

'I wasn't mean,' Marc protested with a grin. 'I was just a normal brother. I'm very fond of Laurette, but you couldn't expect me to tell her that, could you?'

Jane sighed faintly as they left the path and came out on to the verge of the sparkling white gravel road which wound away beneath an avenue of green poplars. Sometimes she felt as if men were some type of bizarre, alien species who had no understanding whatsoever of women's feelings. Was Marc's behaviour really any different now that he was grown up? As a boy he had taken delight in teasing his sister, while now he seemed to derive just as much satisfaction in tormenting and misleading Jane. But what did he really feel towards her? Would she ever know?

'Look, there's the village, up on the hill,' said Marc, interrupting her thoughts.

'Oh, how pretty,' exclaimed Jane.

From a distance it looked like an illustration from a children's book, but as they came closer she saw the details of individual houses with their yellow stucco walls, pale green shutters and orange pantiled roofs which sometimes had incongruously modern TV aerials jutting above them. As they toiled up the steep, cobbled streets several people greeted them from their front doorsteps and each time Jane had to shake hands and be formally introduced. Once a draught horse and cart came clop-clopping down the hill with a creak of leather harness and a rumble of wooden wheels and the driver jumped down with a delighted cry to embrace Marc and shake Jane's hand. By the time they emerged into the square at the top of the hill, Jane felt as if she had met half the village.

Marc waved her into a chair at a table outside the patisserie which had a fine view of the church and belltower on one side and the closely packed houses and shops clinging precariously to the hillside on the other. A smiling woman came out to serve them and there was the inevitable round of introductions, greetings and the exchange of family news before she produced a handwritten menu.

'What will you have?' asked Marc. 'Coffee, bread, pastries?'

'All of them,' said Jane firmly. 'And some orange juice if possible, please. That was quite a climb!'

'But worth it for the view, wouldn't you say?' demanded Marc, waving his hand at the monolithic stone church behind them and the steeply descending view beneath them.

Jane smiled at the unmistakable warmth in his voice.

'You really love this place, don't you?' she asked. He nodded.

'Yes, I do. It's not just the scenery or the buildings, beautiful though they are, but the people! I know they're conservative and sometimes drive me mad, but I like the feeling that it's a community where I belong.'

Jane nodded, feeling vaguely envious. In a way she could say the same thing of her own home in Tasmania, but she had certainly never had the strong family ties that seemed to bind Marc to this place. It was something that she yearned for but didn't really expect to experience. In spite of her envy, or perhaps because of it, she began to bombard Marc with questions about his family and his youth.

His anecdotes were extremely vivid, giving her an unforgettable picture of a closely knit community where work and play were shared against the background rhythm of the seasons. As she watched his eyes light up and saw his mobile features change with the description of past events, Jane felt the insistent tug of attraction more strongly than ever. She loved this man, loved him with a fervour and depth that frightened her. Sitting here in this peaceful village square with him, she could not believe that he was as hardened and cynical as he pretended. Marc Le Rossignol was the product of this community, where people loved and hated and disputed vigorously, where loyalties were deeply felt and emotions still burned white-hot, even after decades. He belonged here and she knew without doubt—but without much hope either—that she wanted to belong with him.

That feeling was only strengthened later in the day by the arrival of the rest of Marc's family for a festive communal lunch. His mother had arranged a single long table in the shade of the trees next to the old château and Jane did her best to earn Brownie points by setting out baskets of bread and bottles of wine, although she hardly dared to handle the beautiful old china and crystal wine glasses which his mother thought appropriate for the meal. When the clan finally gathered, shortly after one o'clock, she was at first taken aback by the exuberant chaos of hugs and shouts and rapid torrents of French. Twelve to one seemed like overwhelming odds, but eventually all the Le Rossignols stopped thumping each other on the back and turned to include her in the uproarious reunion. As Marc drew her into the centre of the circle she tried hard to concentrate and remember everybody's names. Fortunately he spoke in English.

'Jane, I'd like you to meet the rest of my family. My brother Paul and his wife Christine, their two daughters Sophie and Colette and, on the other side, my brother Robert, his wife Monique and their little son Pierre. And this is my sister Laurette, and her fiancé Jacques Dussert. I'd like you all to meet Jane West. Jane's a winemaker and it's possible that I may buy her family vineyard in Australia.'

Jane felt a little twinge of regret as she looked around at all those smiling faces. Everything Marc had said was true, but there was nothing in his words to suggest that she was anything more than a junior colleague in the wine industry. All the same, she thought she saw a speculative gleam of curiosity in the eyes of the women in particular as they stepped forward to shake her hand and kiss her on both cheeks.

There was a strong family resemblance among all the Le Rossignols. Paul and Robert were both as tall as Marc, with similar colouring, although neither of them had his indefinable, brooding animal magnetism. Only Laurette, who was small and dark, with vivid blue eyes like her father's, seemed to share that challenging, sardonic quality. For the present, Jane registered only the simplest details about the others. That Christine was blonde and plump with a good-natured smile and that both her daughters closely resembled her, right down to the elaborate dresses they were wearing. That Monique was tall and dark and elegant, too fully occupied in dealing with a screaming, stiff-backed Pierre to do more than offer Jane a few hasty words of greeting. That Jacques Dussert had copper-coloured curls, an engaging smile and could not take his eyes off Laurette.

'Armand, let us first drink an aperitif and then sit down and eat,' suggested Marc's mother.

At first Jane felt rather overwhelmed, especially since most of the conversation was in French. However, once the meal began, she found herself next to Laurette, who spoke very good English although her accent was a mixture of French and American. Since Marc soon became engaged in an energetic debate with his father and brothers about blending techniques, it was Laurette who translated snippets of conversation for Jane, passed food to her and asked her questions about Australia. She was a lively and amusing companion and, thanks to her tact, Jane soon felt part of the group and was even brave enough to try out a few halting remarks in French.

Before long she found herself relaxing so much that she genuinely enjoyed the ducklings in rich cherry sauce and the apple *galette* that followed. From time to time Marc turned to her with a comment or a question, so that by the time the dessert wines were brought out she was beginning to feel like a member of the family. She felt even more at home when Laurette took pity on the two fidgeting little girls and suggested a game of hide-and-seek in the garden. Most of the adults declined the invitation with a shudder, preferring to sit and sip Sauternes, but Jacques jumped up immediately to join in. Rather to Jane's surprise, Marc also rose lazily to his feet and offered his services to Sophie and Colette.

'Come on, Jane,' he ordered. 'These wicked children can't be trusted on their own. We'll have to play too.'

'Hooray, hooray,' shouted Colette. 'Uncle Marc plays a special kind of hide-and-seek, Jane. He pretends he's a monster, hunting little girls to eat them up.'

It gave Jane an odd, wistful feeling to see how well Marc got along with his nieces. All his sophistication and arrogance seemed to vanish as he stalked them around the shrubbery and outhouses, pouncing on them and sending them running with squeals of terror and delight. What a wonderful father he'd make! thought Jane as a frenzied little girl came running out of the bushes and hurtled headlong into her, almost knocking her down, with Marc in roaring, looming pursuit. Hugging the child, Jane chuckled reproachfully.

'Stop it, Marc!' she protested. 'You'll give her nightmares.'

'Rubbish! She loves it,' he replied, his eyes twinkling.

For a moment they stood gazing, laughing at each other over Colette's head. A current of warmth and understanding seemed to flow between them and Jane felt a surge of hope that the rift between them might soon be healed. Then abruptly the expression on Marc's face changed, as if he had seen something over Jane's shoulder. Instantly he was his old self again. Suave, cool, faintly mocking.

'Well, look who's here,' he said softly.

Jane swung round, following the direction of his gaze, and gave a soft gasp of dismay.

'Simone!' she breathed.

It was as if the sun had just gone in behind a cloud and a chill shadow had settled on her skin. It sent a pang of uneasiness through her to watch Marc walk across to Simone and kiss her on both cheeks. She tried to tell herself that this was just normal French courtesy and meant nothing in particular, but the rest of the family also seemed to be greeting Simone eagerly, as if she was a frequent guest. Only Laurette showed an unexpected reserve, offering her cheek reluctantly for Simone to kiss and greeting her in a subdued voice that was quite unlike her usual exuberance. A momentary flash of hostility gleamed in Simone's eyes as she caught sight of Jane, but she advanced towards her with her hand outstretched and a disarming smile playing about the corners of her lips.

'Why, Jane,' she said. 'What a surprise! How do you happen to be here?'

'Marc invited me,' retorted Jane defiantly.

Simone's plucked eyebrows arched at that and she turned to Marc with a humorously indulgent expression on her face.

'What a good idea, *chéri*,' she said. 'That long flight from Australia is unspeakably dull and exhausting, so I think you were very wise to bring a companion to lessen the tedium. Besides, it will be nice for Jane to see a little more of the world before she goes home.'

This made Jane feel as if she were some kind of X-rated video, guaranteed to offer a brief escape from boredom, but Marc scarcely seemed aware of any insult to her in Simone's words. A thoughtful frown came over his face and he turned to his parents.

'You must excuse Simone and me,' he said abruptly. 'We've got some very important matters to talk about which may take a long time to sort out. I think we'd better go inside at once. If you can keep Jane occupied for me, I'd be grateful.'

'Of course they can,' muttered Jane under her breath. 'Laurette and Jacques can play hide-and-seek with me.'

She caught Laurette's glance of startled amusement, and realised that Marc's sister must have heard her words. Surprisingly the other girl intervened on Jane's behalf.

'Can't your business discussions with Simone wait, Marc?' she asked mildly. 'Jane's come such a long way to visit us that it seems a pity to spoil her time here with financial matters.'

Jane gave Laurette a brief, grateful smile. It was kind of Marc's sister to support her, and doubly tactful to hint that his discussion with Simone would be purely financial in nature. All the same, her intervention did no good. Marc simply gave his sister a weary sidelong look, as if she were an ignorant child interfering in adult affairs.

'It can't be helped,' he said dismissively. 'Simone and I have urgent matters to discuss. You will have to excuse us.'

'*Mon Dieu!*' exclaimed Marc's mother. 'At least let poor Simone have a glass of wine before you carry her off, Marc.'

Simone gave a small, triumphant smirk as she sat down with a glass of Sauternes, but Marc's impatience was obvious. All the while that she sat tranquilly sipping her wine he was drumming his fingers on the table, and the moment she swallowed the last drop he rose to his feet.

'We may be occupied for several hours,' he announced. 'So it's probably best if I say goodbye to you all now. Thank you for coming—it was good to see you again.'

That was a signal for a general move, as Christine and Monique also began to murmur that they must get home. Soon they were all on their feet, rounding up children and retrieving scattered belongings. A cold, aching sense of misery settled in the pit of Jane's stomach as she watched the ritual of kisses and handshakes being repeated. To her surprise, as she stood gazing unhappily after them, Laurette touched her on the shoulder and smiled.

'Jacques and I are staying here overnight,' she said. 'And I'd like to get to know you a little better. Won't you come to my room and have some more coffee?'

'Thank you,' replied Jane gratefully. 'But shouldn't we help your mother with the washing up?'

Madame Le Rossignol clicked her tongue.

'Don't worry about it, child,' she urged. 'Marie has a girl coming up from the village this afternoon to help her. They'll take care of it together. You go away and talk to Laurette.'

Laurette led the way through the eighteenth-century part of the château into a huge, beautifully proportioned room overlooking the terrace and the vineyards beyond. The walls were exquisitely decorated with almond-green and white plasterwork, while the heads and feet of the two vast canopied beds were carved to match. Yet Laurette treated her sumptuous surroundings quite casually.

'Take off your shoes and relax,' she invited. 'Just because this place looks like a museum, you don't have to behave as though you're in church. Lie on one of the beds and get comfortable. That's what I'm going to do as soon as I've made the coffee.'

She crossed to one of the beautifully carved wardrobes built into one wall and flung open the doors, revealing a complete miniature kitchen with gas ring, sink, refrigerator and a cupboard full of supplies. A moment later the aroma of ground coffee beans filled the air as she screwed the percolator together.

'Are you sure I'm not intruding on your time with your fiancé?' asked Jane, obediently kicking off her shoes and perching on one of the beds.

'Of course you're not,' said Laurette with a grin. 'Jacques is planning to go fishing tonight. He says it helps to keep his mind off other things when we're staying here. Even though we share an apartment in Nantes, my mother practically had a heart attack when I suggested we should sleep together here. She's totally medieval in her outlook.'

'Oh, no!' exclaimed Jane in a worried tone. 'I had a feeling we might be offending her. Marc and I——'

She broke off, suddenly realising that it might be more discreet to say nothing, but Laurette's eyes were dancing.

'I know!' she announced in a stage whisper. 'Maman told me the dreadful secret of how you were sleeping together in one of the tower rooms. Well, Marc's more ruthless than I am, so he probably just rode over her feeble cries of opposition. But, I have to warn you, she's expecting a wedding announcement any day now to make it all right.'

Jane flinched.

'Is she really?' she asked in horror. 'Your poor mother. How embarrassing! Look, I might as well tell you the truth, Laurette. Marc and I have had a fight and I've moved out of his room. Besides, even when we were sleeping together he never said anything to me to suggest that it was serious.'

'You mean you're not planning to get married?' asked Laurette in a perplexed tone. 'I felt sure that you must be. When I saw you looking at Marc after lunch today I could have sworn you were in love with him.'

A shadow crossed Jane's face.

'That doesn't mean he's in love with me, does it?' she asked bitterly.

Laurette gave her a thoughtful look.

'It must be pretty serious for him to bring you here to stay. He's never done that with any of his other women before, except Simone. And I'm willing to bet that it's ages since he really cared about her. I don't think he ever forgave her for marrying Gilles.'

'You mean Simone is married?' asked Jane in astonishment.

'Not any more,' replied Laurette. 'Her husband was a Grand Prix racing driver and he was killed in an accident several years ago. But if Marc had really loved her, he would have married her by now, wouldn't he? Heaven knows, she's willing enough!'

'When she came to Tasmania she told me they were going to get married!' blurted out Jane.

Laurette's eyes widened.

'Well, it's the first I've heard of it! And I don't believe a word of it. Marc wouldn't be having an affair with you if he was planning to marry Simone, now would he?'

Jane sighed and shook her head.

'I'm not sure,' she admitted.

'But he must have told you something about how he feels towards you!'

'That's just the trouble. He hasn't!' cried Jane passionately. 'I don't know where I stand with him. He's so secretive.'

It was Laurette's turn to sigh and shake her head.

'I guess you're right,' she admitted. 'Marc does tend to clam up about his feelings, but that doesn't mean he hasn't got any. Look, why don't you talk to him, Jane? Tell him how much he's upsetting you. Ask him what he wants from you. Find out where you stand.'

Jane accepted a cup of strong black coffee from Laurette and nodded soberly.

'All right,' she vowed. 'I will.'

Several hours later Jane woke from a troubled doze to hear the sound she had been waiting for on the stone staircase outside her bedroom. The sound of stealthy footsteps going up to Marc's room. It was almost midnight and obviously his conference with Simone was finally over. Her heart lurched wildly at the thought of what she was about to do, but her mind was made up. She couldn't bear the uncertainty any longer, so she intended to follow Laurette's advice. However difficult it might be, she would tell Marc frankly that she loved him and beg him to be equally honest about his feelings for her. Taking a deep breath, she checked herself in the mirror. With her blonde hair rippling around her shoulders and her eyes huge and troubled, she still looked a bit like Little Orphan Annie. But her body under the clinging satin nightgown was unmistakably a woman's body and there was a resolute set to her jaw. If Marc didn't want a serious, committed relationship with her, she was determined to hear the truth from him.

Picking up the trailing hem of her nightdress, Jane
tiptoed up the chilly stone stairs and tapped firmly on
the heavy oak door. There was a long silence, then it
swung open with a creak. But it wasn't Marc who
stood there in the glowing lamplight. It was a woman,
clad in an even flimsier nightdress than Jane's.

'Simone!' breathed Jane.

'Hello,' exclaimed the other woman with an
amused, quizzical look. 'I'm afraid Marc's already in
bed and I was just about to join him. Is there anything urgent that you want?'

CHAPTER EIGHT

JANE passed a thoroughly wretched night. After the first shock of seeing Simone in Marc's bedroom she muttered something incoherent and retreated to her room downstairs, but her disbelief soon gave way to a mixture of fury, outrage and paralysing misery that left her unable to fall asleep for hours. At four a.m. she was still lying in the dark—red-eyed, miserable, and with a pounding headache—totally unable to think what she should do next. Unable to think of anything except the cruel betrayal that Marc had inflicted upon her. At last towards dawn she fell into a restless, turbulent sleep, but was woken shortly after six a.m. by a knock at the door.

'Marc!' she mumbled in a dazed voice. She felt a brief, treacherous thrill of joy at the thought of seeing him, then memory hit her like a sledgehammer. Her spirits plummeted miserably. Although perhaps he had come to offer some explanation . . .

'Come in,' she ordered miserably.

The door creaked open. This time it was not Marc who stood there with a tray of croissants and coffee, but Simone. Jane stiffened, looking at the other woman with an alert, watchful expression.

'What do you want?' she asked suspiciously.

Simone eyed her thoughtfully for a moment, then crossed the room and set down the tray on the bedside cupboard. After that she pulled up a chair and sat down beside Jane with the brisk air of a detective about to interview a barely lucid assault victim.

'I brought you some breakfast,' she said tranquilly. 'Why don't you eat it while you and I have a little talk?'

'What about?'

'Your position here,' said Simone. She snapped on the bedside lamp and looked closely at Jane. 'Poor girl, you've been crying, haven't you?'

'No,' retorted Jane defiantly. 'I just have bags under my eyes until I put my make-up on in the mornings.' She leaned forward and peered equally searchingly at Simone. 'I can see you suffer from the same problem.'

Simone's eyes flashed ominously, but she took a deep breath and forced herself to smile.

'I can't blame you for feeling hostile towards me,' she said. 'This is a difficult situation for both of us. I'm sorry that I embarrassed you last night, but you must make allowances for the fact that Marc and I haven't seen each other for several weeks and our reunions are always rather sizzling in those circumstances. Still, you shouldn't be hurt by it. I'm sure Marc will sleep with you tonight.'

'No, he won't!' flared Jane. 'You may think all this eternal triangle stuff is glamorous and sophisticated, but I don't want a bar of it.'

'So what do you intend to do?' asked Simone softly.

Jane's eyes narrowed to stormy pinpoints of light.

'For a start I intend to tell Marc exactly what I think of his appalling behaviour,' she announced, flinging back the covers and preparing to get out of bed.

Simone caught her arm and restrained her.

'You can do that if you like,' she said. 'But are you sure it's what you want? If you go upstairs to him now, you know very well you'll get agitated, you'll start crying, you'll make a fool of yourself. And that won't impress Marc. You know he'll just look at you with that cool, weary expression of his, won't he? I don't know whether you've realised it, but he doesn't like scenes.'

Jane made a choking sound deep in the back of her throat. Every muscle in her body was shaking with adrenalin, so that she almost craved a violent, angry quarrel, a chance to tell Marc what she thought of him and unload all her anger and grief. But would it do any good? As she saw the faint, mocking smile that flickered over the Frenchwoman's lips she knew that Simone was right. Marc would just give her a look of cool, weary distaste if she burst in on him and made a jealous scene. All she would achieve by it would be to lose even more of her dignity.

'I wish I were a million miles away from here!' she exclaimed passionately.

Simone nodded her head.

'That's not a bad idea, actually,' she said. 'Of course you can stay here if you want to, but is that what you really want?'

'Of course it's not!' cried Jane hotly.

'Then why not go home to Australia?' urged Simone soothingly. 'I can tell Monsieur and Madame Le Rossignol that you had some kind of urgent phone call—perhaps that one of your parents is sick—and I'd be happy to drive you to Brive. The train from there to Paris only takes a little over four hours and I'm sure you could soon get a flight home without any trouble at all.'

'You're just trying to get rid of me!' flared Jane.

Simone shrugged.

'I don't deny it. But you can hardly blame me, can you? It would certainly be easier for me if you left and probably much less painful for you.'

That statement was unanswerable. Jane bit her knuckles and stared unseeingly in front of her. The thought of going to Laurette for advice rose in her mind, but she dismissed it. No, she couldn't face Laurette—couldn't bear to tell her the truth about how badly Marc had hurt her. She would simply dissolve into tears if she tried. Much as she disliked Simone, and hated the solution she was offering, it did seem to be the best way out. And she could always write to the Le Rossignols later to thank them for their hospitality. Suddenly she made up her mind.

'All right, I'll go,' she said bleakly.

'That's very sensible of you,' murmured Simone. 'Look, I'll run upstairs and dress. Then I'll get my car keys and come back for you in . . . shall we say ten minutes?'

Nobody saw them leave the château. Jane kept expecting someone to open a window and shout at them to demand where they were going, but nothing happened. The whole place simply continued to drowse peacefully in the early morning light as Simone's red sports car turned down the white gravel road that led through the avenue of poplars.

The drive to Brive took almost two hours, but Jane remained silent and miserable, gazing out of her window at the countryside that glided by. Her head ached and there was a lump in her throat. Even now she could scarcely believe in Marc's treachery. Fortunately Simone didn't attempt to talk, but concentrated on sending the car speeding along the country roads towards Cahors, where they turned north. Once they reached the Brive railway station Simone was very efficient about parking the car, transporting Jane's luggage and buying her a train ticket. All the same,

Jane rebelled when Simone showed signs of wanting to stay with her until the train left.

'You don't have to stay and make sure I catch it,' she muttered.

Simone's eyebrows rose.

'I'm just being friendly,' she protested.

Jane snorted.

'I appreciate the ride, but there's no need to be hypocritical. We aren't friends, Simone. You want to get rid of me and I'm leaving. That's all there is to it, so let's just say goodbye and leave it at that.'

'All right,' agreed Simone with a shrug. 'Goodbye. And good luck with your vineyard. I don't think Marc will be buying it now.'

'No,' said Jane with a sigh. 'Well, goodbye, Simone. I hope you and Marc will be very happy.'

And that's the biggest lie I've ever told in my life, thought Jane as she watched Simone's elegant figure retreating from the waiting-room. I don't hope they'll be happy; I hope they'll be just as miserable as I am now. A turmoil of anger and jealousy and disbelief surged through her, mingled with more poignant emotions of tenderness and regret. Even now, in spite of the way Marc had treated her, she longed to see him. Gazing around at the sea of strange faces, she felt a sense of total desolation sweep over her, then a sudden movement near the main door of the station caught her eye and her heart almost stopped beating.

It was him! Lean, dark and apparently seething with annoyance as he pushed his way through the crowds that impeded his progress. Then suddenly his eyes met hers and a flare of ruthless triumph lit his face as if he were an eagle sighting its prey. Jane turned to flee, but found her way blocked by a large luggage trolley.

In panic she swung round, looking for another escape route, but found her wrist caught and held.

'Where in the name of God do you think you're going?' demanded Marc. 'Why did Simone bring you here? And where is she?'

'She's gone,' muttered Jane sullenly, answering the easiest of these questions.

Marc's eyes flashed.

'You still haven't told me what the hell you're doing here!' he snarled. 'It's not customary in polite circles for guests to vanish out of the house at six in the morning with all their luggage without a word of explanation to their hosts. I want to know what you're doing here!'

'How did you know where we were?' faltered Jane.

'I heard the car leaving and caught a glimpse of the pair of you. By the time I was up and dressed it was a damned hard job picking up the trail and figuring out where you'd gone. But never mind that. What are you doing here at the railway station?'

Jane fought down a furious impulse to retort that it wasn't customary in polite circles to sleep with two women on alternate nights. Instead, she gave a cool, indifferent shrug.

'I had a phone call from my father,' she lied. 'He told me he'd had a change of heart about the property and he's decided to release my share of the money, so I don't have any problems any more. I want to get home and get all the documents signed before he changes his mind. If you don't want to buy the Saddler's Corner property then I'll probably buy it from my father myself.'

Marc stared at her in horror and disbelief.

'And you intend just to leave like this? Even if your father has had a change of heart, why can't some arrangement be made by telephone or fax machine? My parents are expecting you to stay on here and I wanted to show you more of the country round Bordeaux.'

For an instant Jane was touched by his obvious dismay, but the memory of Simone gloating in the doorway of his bedroom came blazing back at her, and she hardened her heart.

'Well, there's no point in that now, is there?' she retorted coolly. 'Not with the way things are between us.'

Marc frowned.

'You mean because of what happened last night?' he demanded in exasperation. 'Look, that means nothing, Jane. It was so trivial and meaningless! There's no reason to let it spoil our affection for each other.'

Jane's pride was touched on the raw. How could he dismiss the episode with Simone as if it meant no more than a few thoughtless cross words? A surge of anger flooded through her so that she wanted to hit back and hurt him as badly as he had hurt her.

'Affection?' she sneered. 'What affection? You might as well know the truth, Marc.' A sudden inspiration seized her and the words spilled out, fluent and deadly. 'The only reason I ever slept with you was because I was hoping you'd help me to get my vineyard back! So there's no further point in my staying here now, is there?'

Marc went white around the lips and his eyes blazed.

'You bitch,' he breathed. 'You scheming, wanton little bitch.'

'All's fair in love and war,' retorted Jane, tossing her head. 'Well, do you want me to send back your belongings that you left behind in Tasmania? I don't suppose you're likely to go there again yourself.'

Marc gave a short, mirthless laugh.

'I hope to God I never see the place again!' he rasped. 'Or you.'

She had to turn away so that he wouldn't see the gleam of tears in her eyes, but in a moment she had control of herself again. Her voice came out cool and mocking.

'Goodbye, Marc. Or should I say *adieu*?'

Jane arrived home two days later, feeling depressed and exhausted. It was a double shock to hurtle so swiftly from mid-summer in Europe to mid-winter in Tasmania, but the dismal weather matched her mood. She took a taxi from the airport to the farm and got soaked in the brief interval of getting from the vehicle to the back porch. A feeling of desolation gripped her as she watched the red tail-lights of the taxi disappear down the gravel driveway. Although it was not yet five o'clock, it was almost dark. Scarves of grey mist hung about the hills, the sky was the colour of lead, a banshee wind was driving in from the west in gusts and her fingernails were already beginning to turn blue with cold. But worse than the chill weather was the chill in her heart. Gritting her teeth, she unlocked the back door and struggled inside with her suitcases.

The interior of the farmhouse which she had always thought so cosy and welcoming now seemed just as bleak as the sodden landscape outside. She thought a hot bath might be reviving, but when she turned on the taps she remembered that she and Marc had switched off the hot water service before they went away. Well, she would just have to settle for a hot wash and makeshift meal. She boiled the electric kettle twice—the first time so that she could wash her face and hands and the second time to make a cup of tea.

As she sipped the hot, fragrant liquid she realised with a dazed feeling that she had eaten practically nothing for two days. All the way home on the plane she had been too unsettled to feel hungry and even now the thought of food repelled her. Yet her common sense rebelled at the thought of making herself sick on Marc's account.

Padding across to the freezer, she opened the door and scanned the containers that were neatly labelled in Marc's handwriting. Pulling out a small plastic tub of beef stew, she put it in the microwave oven and pressed the button. That was a mistake. The mouth-watering aroma of stewed beef which soon began to fill the room reminded her dramatically of her previous homecoming. She thought of Marc and that turbulent scene in the cellar followed by the candlelit dinner in the middle of the night. At the time she had thought she hated him, but in retrospect the experience had taken on a bittersweet, nostalgic quality.

Well, she should have realised that her initial distrust of him was perfectly well-founded! She ought to be grateful that the penny had finally dropped and she could now see him exactly as he was. Although somehow she didn't feel in the least bit grateful as she sat doggedly eating beef stew all by herself at the kitchen table. Once she had finished, she dropped everything unwashed into the kitchen sink, dragged herself up the stairs and collapsed into bed. Not that she found much relief there either. Throughout the long hours of darkness her ears rang with the noise of airplane engines. The wind rattled the window frames, disturbing her sleep, and even when she did sink into true slumber she found herself besieged by confusing nightmares about Marc and Simone. She woke shortly after eight o'clock to find that it was still raining.

'I must pull myself together,' she said aloud, dragging herself into a sitting position. 'This won't do! However much Marc has hurt me, I've still got work to do and I mustn't give up.'

After a hot shower and some fresh clothes she rummaged in the kitchen in search of breakfast. Once again there were inevitable memories of Marc, since the freezer contained neatly labelled packages of almond croissants, French bread and even frozen coffee beans. Telling herself sternly not to be a wimp, Jane loaded a tray with pastries and coffee and went into the rumpus-room where she lit the wood fire and sat down to gather her wits.

'Let's see,' she said aloud. 'There must be something I should be doing in the winery or the vineyard.'

At this time of year there were always ditches to dig, buildings to be repaired—not to mention the tasks of disinfecting and fertilising soil, replacing stakes and lining up new plants—although the rain made a lot of these jobs impossible. At least with the bad weather Charlie Kendall was hardly likely to show up to work today, which was a relief. Jane didn't feel as if she could face company yet. Perhaps in a few days when the weather improved they could work on the pruning together. In the meantime, at least she could go and tidy the equipment shed.

Once again she was foiled by Marc's obsessive neatness. All the shelves were already tidy, with bags of Rovral and Bayleton lined up on the highest shelves and secateurs, picking buckets, gardening gloves, wire-netting and irrigation pipe down below. There was nothing left for Jane to do, so she would simply have to nerve herself to face the task she had been dreading most of all. Packing up Marc's possessions so that she could post them to him.

It gave her an uncomfortable feeling to enter the large guest bedroom and see the huge bed where she and Marc had slept together after they became lovers. But as she moved about the room, opening wardrobes and drawers, her jangled nerves began to calm a little. Of course it was still upsetting to see the suede jacket and cashmere sweaters, the tailored suits and handmade Italian shoes that Marc had been in the habit of wearing. Even worse was the indefinable aroma of his aftershave lotion, spicy and subtly disturbing, which still seemed to hover in the air. Yet there was nothing really alarming in the room. None of the sort of clutter that Jane always dispersed around her the moment she stayed in a place. No discarded magazines on the floor, no restaurant menus or theatre tickets, cherished for reasons of sloppy sentimentality, no photos of friends... Wait a moment, though!

Jane had been sorting through the neat stacks of maps and tourist brochures in the roll-top desk and suddenly found a yellow folder of photos under her hand. Opening it up, she saw that they were snapshots from the tour which she and Marc had taken of the island's vineyards. Most of them were dated and captioned on the back, although Marc must have been interrupted at the task for a few were still unidentified. Jane's lips pursed wistfully as she saw that there were several excellent photos of herself—sensitive, revealing and very, very skilfully done. There she was grinning impishly down from the back of a horse in the Huon Valley, looking happy and exuberant against the backdrop of the revolving restaurant and thoughtful and professional in the Pipers Brook winery.

The photos of Marc weren't nearly as good. Most of them had been taken by her and were either slightly out of focus or had half his head cut off. Yet there was one of the pair of them together which a Japanese tourist had kindly taken on the dance floor at the Launceston Country Club. Marc was in a dinner suit and Jane was dressed in her green georgette evening frock, but it was the expression on both their faces which stopped her in her tracks. Not so much the look of radiant joy in her eyes, although that made her cringe now, but the expression of brooding tenderness on Marc's face as he gazed down at her.

He did love me! she told herself passionately. He did, at least for a while. Impulsively she snatched up a pen from the desk and turning the photo over scrawled the date and her own caption: 'My darling Marc, even though you broke my heart, I'll always love you. Always, always, always. Jane.'

Then, with a complete revulsion of feeling, she crushed the photo into a ball, flung it down on the floor and uttered an angry groan.

'How can I be so stupid?' she demanded aloud. 'I've got to forget him, not keep wallowing in it! Perhaps if I get rid of all his things, that will make me feel better.'

She began darting around the room, grabbing clothes off hangers and out of drawers, flinging everything on to the bed. Once it was all there in an untidy pile, she went in search of boxes and a roll of masking tape. She had just found the kitchen scissors in the upstairs bathroom, where she had used them to lever the lid off a tin of paint, when the telephone rang. Without much interest, Jane answered it.

'Hello, Jane West speaking.'

'Jane.'

She froze. It was Marc's voice, so close that he sounded as if he were in the room with her.

'I need to talk to you. We have things to discuss.'

'No! We have nothing to discuss!' she cried wildly. 'For heaven's sake, leave me alone, can't you? I never want to see you again in my life!'

Her voice cracked on the last words and she slammed down the phone and held it there as if it were the lid on a manhole that Marc might emerge from at any moment. A shudder went through her.

'I'm going to be calm,' she said very slowly and clearly. 'I'm going to make myself a cup of tea and be very, very calm.'

The kettle in the kitchen had just come to the boil when she heard a knock at the back door. For one absurd moment her heart lurched wildly, as if she expected Marc to walk in at any moment. Then she reminded herself that Marc was in Europe. It was probably only Charlie.

'Come in,' she called listlessly.

There was a shuffling sound as if someone was rearranging belongings. She went to the door and flung it open. It wasn't Charlie, it was Brett—with a newspaper held over his head to keep off the worst of the rain and a loaf of bread and a carton of milk tucked under one arm.

'G'day, Jane,' he said cheerfully. 'Why didn't you tell us you were coming back so soon? I would have brought some proper food in for you. As it was, I saw the smoke from your chimney and thought I'd nip over with some bread and milk.'

With an effort, Jane tried to maintain an air of normality.

'Oh, Brett, how sweet of you. Come inside and get dried off. Tell me, how's Karen?'

Brett stamped his feet on the doormat, tossed the wet newspaper down on the porch and passed the bread and milk to Jane with the dexterity of a keen rugby player.

'Karen's great,' he said, and his face reddened. 'Actually, we're planning to get married.'

'I'm so pleased,' said Jane warmly, forgetting her own troubles for a moment and hugging him.

'How's Marc?' rejoined Brett at last, with the air of someone expecting equal good news.

Jane's face puckered. She clutched at the bread and milk as if she were holding an orphaned baby.

'Oh, Bre-ett!' she wailed.

Ten minutes later Jane's earthquake sobs were subsiding, while Brett was sitting on the rumpus-room couch, dabbing her face with a tea-towel and looking harassed.

'I'll kill that Frenchie if he ever comes back here,' he vowed.

'He won't,' Jane assured him miserably. 'He told me he never wants to see Tasmania again, or me either. Oh, Brett, I'm so unhappy.'

'Now, look, don't start again, love,' urged Brett. 'You'll meet someone else sooner or later, you're bound to.'

'I don't want someone else. I want him! At least . . . What am I saying? Of course I don't want him. I hate him! I'm never going to marry anybody else, though.'

Brett looked troubled.

'You've got to do something with your life,' he argued. 'You'll be lonely if you stay on your own.'

'I want to be lonely,' cried Jane passionately. 'I'm sick of men. Anyway, I've still got my vineyard and my winery—not that I care about that any more. Besides, my rotten father will probably sell the property to someone else.'

'No!' growled Brett, slapping one hand down on his meaty thigh. 'My oath, he won't! I can't help you out with your troubles over that French bloke, Jane, but I can and will help you out over the vineyard. It's not right for your dad to take control of the money that your gran left to you. I'll tell you what you should do—if Marc Lee Russett . . . Lee Rossy——' as usual Marc's name defeated him '—if that Frenchie isn't going to buy Saddler's Corner then you'll have to buy it yourself. At least then you'll have a secure home and a job, even if you never do get married.'

Jane stared at him as if he had suddenly sprouted a second head.

'Buy Saddler's Corner from my father?' she echoed. 'How can I? I haven't any money left, apart from what's already tied up in his company.'

'You haven't, but I have,' retorted Brett. 'I've got a tidy bit put aside and I'll stand as your guarantor so that you can get a bank loan.'

Jane stared at him with a stunned expression.

'You'd really do that for me?' she asked.

'Yeah, of course I would. Reckon it will be a good investment too, one of these days. Mind, you'll have to get a good accountant to do your bookkeeping for you.'

Jane was so touched that she could hardly speak for a moment. When she did, her tears threatened to spill over again.

'Yes, of course,' she said huskily. 'Oh, Brett, you're such a good friend!'

She hugged him violently and he patted her rather nervously on the shoulder.

'Well, don't start crying again,' he warned. 'Let's do something practical instead. We'll get your dad on the blower and tell him you want to buy the property from him. Has the option to purchase expired yet?'

Jane struggled to concentrate.

'I think so, but I'm not really sure. In any case, it can't run for much longer, and I'm quite certain Marc doesn't want the property now. Oh, go on, Brett, ring Dad up and let's get it over with.'

Jane found the number and Brett dialled it, then handed her the phone. She took a deep breath and tried to nerve herself for the lengthy confrontation which seemed bound to follow. To her amazement the discussion proved unexpectedly short. When Jane dropped the receiver and turned back to Brett her eyes were wide and her cheeks ashen.

'What is it?' demanded Brett sharply.

'It's too late,' she whispered. 'Marc's already bought the place.'

CHAPTER NINE

JANE felt a stab of pain as the full cruelty of Marc's action struck home. Could he really be so spiteful as to punish her for leaving him by buying her home and expelling her on to the street? The vindictiveness of it took her breath away, even though she had already had ample opportunity to witness Marc's callous ruthlessness in other ways. While she was still sitting stunned and speechless, Brett burst hotly into an impassioned outpouring of threats and protests and plans for revenge. A strange, unnatural calm seemed to descend on Jane and she put up her hand to halt his flow of words.

'It's all right, Brett,' she said with a coolness that astonished her. 'I'm very grateful for all that you've done, but I don't want to fight this. I simply don't care any more. I'll just pack up my things and go quietly when the time comes for Marc to take over the property. Not that he's likely to appear in person to claim it in any case.'

'But where will you go? What will you do?' demanded Brett indignantly. 'It's not right!'

Jane shrugged.

'I don't care about the money or the property any more,' she said wearily. 'And I'm sure I can find a job somewhere. Perhaps at one of the mainland vineyards.'

'Look, mate——' began Brett.

'No, Brett,' she insisted firmly. 'Let it drop, please. I'm going to be all right.'

175

Her resolve carried her through till the weekend when she drove into Richmond and returned with the national newspaper that carried the job advertisements.

The series of cold fronts had vanished across the Tasman Sea and the weather was now deceptively mild and tranquil. Looking around at the bright gold sunshine and the cloudless blue sky, Jane could almost have believed that it was late spring if it had not been for the bare vines which stood in stark rows on every hillside around the farmhouse. They would need pruning soon, but that would not be her problem. With a sigh she pulled up the car on the gravel turning circle, switched off the ignition and went inside the house. She had just settled at the dining-room table and was busily scanning the job advertisements when she heard the sound of another car coming up the driveway. The engine revs died away, footsteps crunched on the gravel. Jane walked slowly to the back door and turned the handle.

'Is that you, Bre——? Oh!'

Everything seemed to spin around her so that the universe broke up into extraordinarily vivid fragments. Sunlight gleaming on dewy leaves, the scent of wet daphne, the immaculate cut and soft texture of Marc's suede jacket, the elegant crispness of his beige trousers, light green shirt and autumn-toned tie. It was Marc, there could be no question of that, although Jane couldn't really believe she was seeing him. She took a step backward and caught her breath.

'What are you doing here?' she demanded resentfully. 'Have you come to throw me out?'

He took his time about answering, letting his gaze travel over her with insulting completeness. His brown eyes were narrowed and glittering and there was a bitter twist to his mouth. To her annoyance he pushed past her as if he owned the place—well, he did, didn't he? Or soon would!—and took up his stance behind one of the dining-chairs.

'No, quite the reverse,' he said in a clipped voice as he tossed an important-looking document down on the table. 'I've come to give you the title deed of the property. Take it!'

Jane's features creased in bewilderment.

'I—I don't understand,' she stammered.

Marc sucked in breath impatiently.

'It's simple enough,' he snapped. 'I bought the property in your name, so I'm giving you the title deeds.'

'Saddler's Corner?' she echoed. 'You bought Saddler's Corner in my name?'

'Yes.'

'Why?' gasped Jane.

'Because I didn't like the thought that your father might turn you out if I left him in possession of the place. However much you and I hate each other, I owe you something, Jane.'

Jane flinched at the venom in his tone and turned away from him with a blind, despairing movement.

'You don't have to pay me for having sex with you,' she said ,in an unsteady voice.

Marc strode around to rejoin her and seized her by the chin, forcing her to look up at him. She saw that his nostrils had a pinched look and his mouth was set in a hard line.

'Oddly enough, it's not the sex I'm "paying" for, if that's how you choose to put it!' he said harshly. 'You gave me something much greater than sex and I want to offer you something in return.'

Jane's throat hurt so badly that she could scarcely utter the words.

'What did I give you?' she demanded.

A shadow crossed Marc's face, but he continued to gaze down at her.

'Your virginity, with all that that implies,' he muttered. 'Innocence. Trust. Love? I feel I owe you something for that.'

Jane caught her breath at the burning mixture of hatred and tenderness in his eyes. When she spoke her voice was sharp with sarcasm, and the words came out like a hail of bullets.

'And my *innocence*, my *trust*, my *love* really meant a lot to you, didn't they?' she flared.

'Oddly enough, they did,' replied Marc coldly. 'Until you betrayed and deserted me.'

'I betrayed and deserted you? You've got a nerve saying that after the way you treated me!'

Marc's eyes narrowed.

'I don't know what the hell you mean,' he said through his teeth. 'My conscience is perfectly clear. Still, there's no point staying here, trading insults with you. Just take the title deed, sign the document from my lawyer and I'll be on my way.'

Jane pushed past him to the table, picked up the title deed and tried to thrust it back into his hands.

'I don't want it!' she shouted. 'I don't care about the vineyard any more.'

'That's not what you told me in France,' snarled Marc.

'I don't care what I told you in France. You think you can come here and clear your conscience about what you did with Simone by paying me off, don't you? Well, you're wrong! No amount of property or money could ever compensate me for the way you hurt me and I won't take anything from you. Now, get out, will you? Get out and leave me alone! You've already ruined my life, isn't that enough for you?'

Marc stared at her with a baffled expression.

'What I did with Simone,' he repeated softly. 'Just what exactly did I do with Simone, according to you?'

'Do I have to spell it out for you?' cried Jane. 'You know damn well what you did! You slept with her the night before I left France.'

Marc shook his head in a dazed fashion.

'Are you crazy, Jane? I did nothing of the kind!' he protested.

It was Jane's turn to look shocked and disbelieving. Then the evidence of her own eyes came flashing vividly back to her.

'Don't lie to me!' she shouted. 'I went up to your room the night before I left and Simone came to the door in her nightdress. She said you were already in bed.'

Marc swung round and slammed both fists down on the dining-table with a thunderous crash.

'I wasn't in my room at all that night. I was out fishing with Jacques!' he roared.

Jane's heart began to beat frantically and her breath came in shallow, uneven gulps as she stared at Marc with a tormented expression. She wanted to believe him, wanted it more than she had ever wanted anything in her life. Yet she could not quite banish the tormenting suspicion that he was just making a fool of her once again.

'Well, why would Simone say that you were?' she demanded.

Their eyes met and there was a long silence as they both drew the same conclusions. At last Marc gave a deep, shuddering sigh.

'Because she wanted me herself,' he muttered. '*Mon Dieu*, what a fool I've been! To think I believed Simone's assurances that she liked you and wished us both well... Jane, why did you come to my room that night?'

Jane wanted to lie, to protect her pride, to hold on to some shred of concealment, but Marc's brooding dark eyes seemed to strip her totally naked and there was a husky, caressing warmth in his voice which hadn't been there before.

'I was going to tell you that I loved you,' she said hoarsely. 'And ask you whether you felt anything at all for me.'

A tear trembled on her lashes and slid quietly down her cheek. She gulped and wiped it away. Suddenly she found herself crushed in Marc's arms.

'Oh, my love, my love,' he said thickly. 'What a pair of fools we've been! Is it too late to tell you that I love you with all my heart?'

Joy, hope and disbelief swept over Jane like a tidal wave.

'Marc, don't make fun of me!' she begged. 'I can't bear any more deceit.'

'I do love you, Jane,' he insisted, tilting her chin so that he could look into her brimming green eyes. 'I love you as I've never loved any woman in my life before and as I'll never love any woman again.'

She gazed at him in torment, longing to believe him but unable to lay her past suspicion and mistrust so easily aside.

'Then why didn't you tell me so before?' she demanded.

Marc sighed and put up one hand to scratch his head.

'I was fighting it,' he admitted. 'I hadn't been in love since I was nineteen, and this was so much more intense, so much more profound, so much more real that it frightened me. I didn't want to be made so vulnerable.'

'Who were you in love with when you were nineteen?' asked Jane.

He looked down at her with a wry smile.

'I think you already know that, don't you?' he said softly.

'Simone?' she asked, feeling a barb of pain go through her.

He nodded ruefully.

'What happened?' she asked.

'Everything,' said Marc with a shrug. 'Or nothing, depending on how you look at it. Do you really want to know?'

Jane hesitated. Did she? It caused her unbelievable pain to think of Marc being in love with another woman, especially Simone, but it was important for her to know what had happened if she was ever really to understand him.

'Yes,' she insisted.

Marc released his hold on her and paced around the room.

'I was nineteen and a university student when it happened,' he said in a flat, unemotional voice. 'I came home for the grape harvest and on the night of the harvest festival Simone and I ended up having too much to drink. It was a warm evening and ... At first we were just lying in the thick grass on a hillside, kissing under the stars and then ... It was my first experience of sex and that's such a primal force that I found myself shaken to the core. I told Simone that

I loved her, that I wanted to marry her and she assured me that she felt the same way.'

Marc trailed off as if lost in thought.

'And after that?' prompted Jane.

'I had to go back to university in Paris, but when I went home again that Christmas I was determined to make some kind of formal declaration of my commitment to Simone. I had an engagement ring I intended to give her but, when I arrived at her house, at first I couldn't get her alone. In particular a racing car driver called Gilles Boutin seemed to be hanging about her. He was years older than her, in fact he must have been about thirty-seven or thirty-eight, so I didn't take much notice because I thought he was a friend of her parents. Then I saw that Simone was already wearing a ring on her left hand, a far finer ring than mine. She told me that she and Gilles had just become engaged.'

Jane's eyes widened, although thanks to Laurette's revelation the news did not really surprise her. All the same she felt a rush of sympathy for Marc in his youth.

'How did you feel?' she asked softly.

'At the time I was devastated, but that only lasted for a few days. Gradually I realised that it was not the loss of Simone that wounded me so much as the loss of my pride. Looking back now, I don't think it was ever really love that I felt for her, but only a boy's infatuation. Eventually I even came to feel grateful to her for rejecting me.'

'Why?' asked Jane with a puzzled frown.

'Because I was still a romantic at heart. If I was ever going to marry, I wanted my wife to be in love with me body and soul. And Simone wasn't. Even after Gilles's death, when she made it perfectly clear that she would be willing to marry me, I was sure it was only because I had become a wealthy man in the meantime. I preferred to stay a bachelor rather than settle for a relationship as empty as that!'

'Didn't you ever think of marrying anyone else?'

'No. Because I never met anyone who lit up a room when she came into it, anyone who made me ecstatic and miserable at the same time, who drove me crazy and made me feel I couldn't live without her. Until I encountered you.'

Jane gave a long, shaky sigh. She had almost succeeded in convincing herself that Marc had only had an affair with her out of careless sensual exuberance. To learn that he wasn't in love with Simone had come as a major shock. To hear him admit that Jane herself had stirred him so deeply was almost more than she could believe.

'Do you mean that?' she asked shakily.

Marc sighed and nodded.

'Yes, I mean it. Not that I was really very grateful when it happened. By that time I had become used to being a bachelor and I wasn't sure that I wanted to be so much in anybody else's power, so I fought my attraction to you all the way. When you told me that first time we slept together that you loved me, it made me feel like the king of the universe. I wanted to protect you and cherish you and claim possession of you forever. At the same time your words filled me with terror. What if I lost you or you changed your mind as Simone did? What if it was only the newness of the experience which had deceived you about your own feelings? Because of what had happened in my own life, I knew what a powerful, overwhelming experience that first time could be. I was afraid you might be saying things that you would regret later and I had to bite my tongue to stop myself from rushing you and proposing then and there. At the same time, I couldn't bear to let you go. That's why I asked you to come to France with me, so that I could find out whether you really were as desperately in love with me as I was with you.'

'I wish I'd known!' cried Jane. 'I was so miserable, thinking that you were just having an idle affair with me. Simone told me that you were in the habit of sleeping with young women for a few weeks at a time, just for fun.'

Marc caught his breath sharply.

'That lying——! Well, never mind her. I wanted you to see me in my own environment in France, to see if you felt you could fit in there. I was half dismayed, half relieved when you didn't seem to like the place at all.'

'I did like it!' protested Jane. 'What I didn't like was the feeling that I would never belong there. I wanted to belong so badly, to be your wife, to be part of your family. I wanted you to love me and make a public commitment to me.'

Marc scowled at her with mock ferocity.

'That's not what you told me in the railway station at Brive,' he reminded her. 'You said that you'd only been sleeping with me to try and get your vineyard back. So what have you got to say to that, *mademoiselle*?'

'I lied,' admitted Jane remorsefully. 'I wanted to hurt you just as badly as you'd hurt me. I couldn't bear to think of you sleeping with Simone.'

Marc caught her by the hair and hauled her against him.

'I ought to tan the hide off you, Jane,' he threatened, gazing down at her through narrowed brown eyes. 'How could you think such a thing of me? I certainly didn't bring Simone to the château in order to go to bed with her.'

'Why did you bring her there?' asked Jane with a puzzled expression.

'There really were a lot of financial details that needed to be sorted out,' explained Marc. 'For a long time my parents had felt that the upkeep of the château was too much of a burden for them. The French inheritance laws are so complicated that if they died then all of us children would inherit it jointly. None of the others really want it, so I thought it was best to make arrangements to buy the place outright from my parents. My own life seemed to be on the brink of a major change and I wanted to make sure that all the financial details were tidied up.'

Jane's lips began to twitch.

'Trust you to want things tidy,' she said accusingly. 'But I think you're going to have to get a new accountant in future, Marc.'

'I agree,' said Marc. 'In fact I've already made it very clear to Simone that I want nothing to do with her in future.'

'Hmm,' said Jane, returning to his previous statement. 'What sort of change are you contemplating in your life, Marc?'

His eyes crinkled with amusement.

'I'm thinking of getting married,' he said in measured tones. 'And I hope to have a lot of children, so I'll need plenty of space to accommodate them. That's why I thought the château would be a suitable home.'

'Marc, there are sixty-seven rooms in that château,' said Jane faintly.

His arms tightened around her.

'Mmm,' he murmured. 'We're going to have to start work soon if we want to fill them all.'

The gleam in his eyes vanished and he was suddenly earnest. Jane's heart began to beat violently as she realised that he was about to ask the question that she had longed to hear. And then he did.

'Will you marry me, Jane? Will you be my wife and the mother of my children?'

Jane rose on tiptoe and gave him a long, inviting kiss.

'Of course I will,' she said.

Marc drew back to look at her and his breath was coming in harsh, uneven gulps. His hands gripped her shoulders so tightly that it hurt, but she didn't care. All she cared about was the look of dawning elation on his face, the fierce, incredulous joy that made him utter a sudden shout of triumph.

'Yes! Yes! *Mon Dieu* . . . you have made me the happiest man in Australia. What am I saying? In Australia? In the world! I am king of the world at this moment, Jane. And you—you are my queen.'

With a movement so sudden that it took her by surprise, he swept her off her feet and stood gazing intently down at her. Then his mouth came down on hers in a kiss that told her all she needed to know. There had been passion between them in the past, and anger and a wordless need, but never this deep, aching tenderness. Marc's kiss was urgent, hungry, demanding, but it was also giving in a way that was new to her. No longer did he hold aloof from her, no longer did she sense a hidden reserve or tension in his feelings towards her. Instead he kissed her with all the intensity of a stormy, emotional nature held too long in check. At last he drew free and caught his breath.

'I love you!' he insisted. 'I love you, I love you, I love you, Jane. It makes me burn and ache and shudder with need for you. And I want you to feel the same way about me.'

'I do,' she whispered.

'Then say it! Tell me.'

'I love you, Marc.'

Her voice was low and rather shy, but it had the ring of truth. Marc gave a low growl of triumph, and his arms tightened around her like steel cables.

'Then nothing will save you now, *mademoiselle*,' he warned. 'Or should I say "*madame*"? Because very soon I intend to make you Madame Le Rossignol, my wife and the mother of my children. And it is as my future wife that I want to take you to my bed this very moment and make you mine. With no lies, no misunderstanding, no doubts to spoil it. But with trust. With honour. With eternal love between us. Do you agree?'

Jane was so moved that she could scarcely speak. She gazed up at him with her emotions brimming in her eyes and a small, tremulous smile playing about the corners of her lips.

'Yes,' she said huskily.

He planted another feverish kiss on her lips, then strode swiftly out of the door and along the hall to his old bedroom. Impatiently he kicked the door shut behind him and flung Jane down in the middle of the vast bed. Lying beside her, he caught her hair in handfuls and bunched it on either side of her face.

'You are so beautiful,' he breathed. 'So very, very beautiful. I love you more than I can ever tell you.'

He gazed down at her with an intent, brooding expression, almost as if he wanted to devour her.

Reaching up, she trailed her forefinger down his left cheek.

With a slow, deliberate sensuality he began unbuttoning her shirt and then coolly undid the front fastening of her bra. Her breasts sprang free from their confinement and Marc bent his head and nuzzled the warm soft flesh, inhaling the scent of her skin. Then, with the same deliberate, provocative intentness, he took one of her nipples between his fingers and slipped it into his mouth. She closed her eyes and moaned softly with pleasure at the tingling, throbbing sensation of delight that shot through her as he began to suck. He was in no hurry, but let her arch her back and thresh from side to side, gasping and offering herself to him, before he paused briefly. Then he renewed the wanton thrill of the act by repeating it on her other breast. Only when she was shuddering and whimpering, alternately pushing him away and clutching him against her, did he take pity on her.

'Are you ready?' he murmured.

'Yes,' she whispered. 'Oh, yes, Marc. My love, my darling.'

He made a harsh sound deep in the back of his throat and sprang to his feet. With impatient wrenching movements he tore off his clothes and flung them aside. Then he crouched above her on the bed, looming over her with an urgency that made her heart thud in a frantic, uneven rhythm. His eyes met hers, dark and compelling and full of unspoken need.

She reached out to him and gave a deep sigh of contentment as she found herself crushed beneath that hot, hard, virile body. There would be time enough for lingering love games on other occasions. This time she wanted him violently, wanted him now—deep and urgent and thrusting inside her. With trembling fingers she reached for him, caressing him intimately, guiding him into her warm, moist, feminine core. She heard his gasp of satisfaction as he entered her and her body moved, slick and quivering, to meet him.

'I love you, Marc,' she murmured.

His hands caught in her hair, his eyes narrowed and his lips came down on hers—demanding, giving, sharing.

'I love you too, Jane,' he said thickly.

As their bodies began to move together as one she clasped her arms around his neck and surrendered to a happiness too deep for words. All her worries and problems were over. Marc was really here. He loved her—he was going to marry her. And he was no longer an unwelcome invader, but her man. Her own beloved man. Sometimes life was so perfect, it was enough to make a girl cry.

TASTY FOOD COMPETITION!

How would you like a years supply of Temptation books ABSOLUTELY FREE? Well, you can win them! All you have to do is complete the word puzzle below and send it in to us by 31st October 1995. The first 5 correct entries picked out of the bag after that date will win a years supply of Temptation books (*four books every month - worth over £90*). What could be easier?

```
H O L L A N D A I S E R
E Y E G G O W H A O H A
R S E E C L A I R U C T
B T K K A E T S I F I A
E E T I S M A L C F U T
U R C M T L H E E L Q O
G S I U T F O N O E D U
N H L S O T O N E F M I
I S R S O M A C W A A L
R I A E E T I R J A E L
E F G L L P T O T V R E
M O U S S E E O D O C P
```

CLAM	HOLLANDAISE	OYSTERS	SPICE
COD	JAM	PRAWN	STEAK
CREAM	LEEK	QUICHE	TART
ECLAIR	LEMON	RATATOUILLE	
EGG	MELON	RICE	
FISH	MERINGUE	RISOTTO	
GARLIC	MOUSSE	SALT	
HERB	MUSSELS	SOUFFLE	

PLEASE TURN OVER FOR DETAILS ON HOW TO ENTER ➡

HOW TO ENTER

All the words listed overleaf, below the word puzzle, are hidden in the grid. You can find them by reading the letters forward, backwards, up or down, or diagonally. When you find a word, circle it or put a line through it, the remaining letters (which you can read from left to right, from the top of the puzzle through to the bottom) will ask a romantic question.

After you have filled in all the words, don't forget to fill in your name and address in the space provided and pop this page in an envelope (you don't need a stamp) and post it today. Hurry – competition ends 31st October 1995.

Temptation Tasty Food Competition,
FREEPOST,
P.O. Box 344,
Croydon,
Surrey. CR9 9EL

Hidden Question _____

_____

Are you a Reader Service Subscriber? Yes ☐ No ☐

Ms/Mrs/Miss/Mr _____

Address _____

_____

_____ Postcode _____

One application per household.

You may be mailed with other offers from other reputable companies as a result of this application. Please tick box if you would prefer not to receive such offers. ☐